Fiction
McCreede, Jess
Colorado ambush

REBEL'S VENGEANCE

Hunter felt the rush of air that passed by him as he rolled from his bed to the floor, pulling his Colt out from beneath his pillow. Bringing the gun to full cock, he heard a muffled curse and saw the shadowy knife-wielding figure that loomed above him. Hunter fired once, then a second time. The figure let out a strangled cry and crashed backward into the washstand.

Cautiously Hunter moved to the window and pushed aside the curtains for more light. He could see the intruder sprawled on the floor, his face pale and drawn with blood seeping from a corner of his mouth. A large crimson circle spread slowly outward from the center of his chest.

"Never figgered no Yankee eastern dude could take me," the dying man said weakly. "'Specially one who worked for Grant."

Hunter was stunned. "Who are you? How did you know that?" he demanded. "I want to know who told you that!"

The dying man managed a half-smile filled with pain, his eyes blazing with pure hatred. "Bet you would, Yank," he said, his voice trailing off to a whisper. "I may be outa the game, but this party's far from over."

COLORADO AMBUSH

Jess McCreede

PINNACLE BOOKS
WINDSOR PUBLISHING CORP.

PINNACLE BOOKS

are published by

Windsor Publishing Corp.
475 Park Avenue South
New York, NY 10016

First printing: February, 1989

Printed in the United States of America

To Jack M. Bickham . . .
who lit the fires,
and to Sylvia and Brenda,
who kept them going

AUTHOR'S NOTE

On August 3, 1864, at Union headquarters, City Point, Virginia, an ordnance boat exploded by Confederate spies killed forty-three men and wounded forty. A short distance away, General-in-Chief Ulysses S. Grant barely escaped injury, and his camp staff realized how vulnerable he was to assassination. To prevent this, each staff officer took his turn standing guard over Grant's tent every night thereafter. They called themselves "Watchers" and General Grant knew nothing of this dedicated group until his second term as president.

This story concerns one member of the Watchers as he provides secret service protection for President Grant on his visit to Colorado in 1873.

Several historical figures play minor roles in this story in addition to President Grant: John Routt, later to become Colorado's first governor; Belle Siddons, a Southern spy who operated a successful tent saloon as Madame Vestal in Denver; Thomas C. Durant, Grenville Dodge, and Sidney Dillon, all of the Union Pacific Railroad; Henry Teller of the Colorado Central Railroad; and Richard "Uncle Dick" Wootton, trailblazer, trapper, and mountain man extraordinary. Historians should overlook the deliberate extension of Wootton's stay in Denver.

The reference to Jack Reynolds's hidden gold in Handcart Gulch still persists to this day.

It is true a sidewalk of silver ingots (at the time valued at $13,000) from the Caribou Mine was laid in front of the Teller House in Central City for President Grant to walk across in April 1873.

7

CHAPTER ONE

They worked the cattle before the gathering storm building between the craggy peaks to the west. James Hunter looked up from the small fire at the ominous thick clouds rolling toward them, unbroken and low. He picked up the branding iron and walked back to where a big yearling lay struggling against a leather string and pressed the iron against the calf's red fur. The calf let go with a loud bawl and renewed his fight against the rawhide. Hunter slipped the pigging string from the animal and watched as he raced back to the far side of the corral with tail held high.

Whip Shorely rode up dragging another protester for Hunter to brand, and he quickly tied the kicking animal with the piece of rawhide.

"Storm coming," Whip said, pausing to wipe the sweat from his dusty face as he eased the tension on the rope so Hunter could slip the noose from the animal. Hunter slowly straightened, feeling his back muscles protest like overworked springs. He looked up at the old prospector-turned-cowhand now coiling the leather lariat before shifting his eyes once more to the approaching storm. A slight breeze drifting down from the higher meadow was like a cooling drink to Hunter's fire-burned face.

"Guess the warm spell is over," Hunter replied as he carried the iron back to the fire and picked up another that outlined the "Rocking H" in dull red.

"That's the last in this bunch. Hafta start working the higher draws tomorrow . . . if we can," Whip added as an afterthought, looking again at the line of slate-gray snow clouds. Hunter made short work of the calf and released him to join the others.

"Turn'm out, Whip, they'll not head back into rough country with this storm brewing. Besides, there's plenty of good forage and shelter here by Sun Creek to keep them from straying far."

Whip Shorely turned his tired black toward the gate without comment and hazed the thirty-odd head of prime livestock out while Hunter gathered up the irons and kicked dirt over the small fire.

For the past week Hunter and Shorely had taken advantage of the unusually warm weather that had pushed the snow line deeper into the higher elevations and thick-forested slopes, to begin the spring roundup early. But there was another, more pressing reason for them to finish branding as soon as possible. One Hunter had not mentioned to Shorely.

Hunter recinched the saddle on his big buckskin and climbed aboard. It felt good to sit down again after spending the day scrambling around on the dusty ground.

"Rider coming," Whip barked as he rode up beside Hunter. They studied the approaching figure for a full minute. He was a good mile off and unrecognizable.

"May as well save him the full trip, seeing as how we are headed that way," Hunter said. Shorely closed the corral gate behind them.

The corral was located in a high-sloping meadow bisected by Sun Creek, while to either side were broken hills heavily forested with aspen and spruce. Some two miles away, near the confluence of the Sun and Gunnison rivers, lay the modest spread Hunter had begun the spring before. Whip Shorely joined him that summer after a season of unsuccessful prospecting. Stove-up and arthritic, Shorely needed a place to ride out the winter, and Hunter needed help in getting his cattle down out of the high country before the snows closed the passes. The arrangement benefited both men, yet Shorely knew he had gotten the better deal. Shorely threw himself into his work with plenty of grit determination . . . and, what Hunter valued most, experience.

A one-time horse rancher near the Brazos River before Yankees burned him out during the war, Whip Shorely didn't know much about prospecting but he did know ranching and

10

he put this knowledge to good use. Hunter valued the old man's help and wondered how he ever got along without him.

They were half a mile apart when Shorely spoke. "That's Gabe Pitts, from down Lake City way. Worked a claim next to mine down on Henson crick last year. We both rode away broke. Wonder what brings him out this way?" Whip pulled his hat lower on his head as the first few flakes of snow and ice from the leading edge of the storm pelted them. Hunter didn't know for sure why Pitts was here, but he had an idea. He was expecting something like this, and it couldn't come at a worse time.

Gabe Pitts reined in and waited for the approaching horsemen.

"Figgered to find you boys up here after stopping by your place," Gabe Pitts said as they rode up.

"Why Gabe Pitts, you old coon, what flushed you outen them mountains?" Shorely asked as the two prospectors shook hands.

"Howdy, Whip. Man's gotta come down now and again even if it ain't fer nuthin' but beans and coffee anymore."

"Gabe, meet Jim Hunter. Owns this here spread." Gabe felt the strength beneath Hunter's grip. Hunter found himself being measured by pale eyes from beneath a grease-stained hat. He was accustomed to frank, open appraisals of men like Pitts, Western men bred of hard times, where friendships sometimes meant dying together. A man had to learn to form quick judgments of those around him. His life could depend on these evaluations. Pitts liked what he saw in Hunter. The steel-gray eyes and quiet resolve spoke of a man sure of himself and his surroundings.

Hunter saw a lean-framed man with a deep-seamed face like weathered granite. A large mustache covered his upper lip and matched the graying hair that stuck from beneath the floppy hat. Pitts was rawhide tough, characteristic of their breed, who survived most times on short rations and hard work.

"Kinda early to be working cattle, ain't it?" Pitts asked Hunter.

"This country a man's gotta work around the weather," Hunter said.

11

"Yeah, know what you mean." Pitts pulled his coat closer about him. The icy wind was biting cold. Know you boys are tired, so I'll cut short the palaver." Pitts fished in a coat pocket and brought out a wrinkled telegram which he handed to Hunter.

Hunter could feel his heart beating heavily against his ribs. He didn't need to read it to know what it contained . . . he knew the words by heart. This wire confirmed dates mentioned in a wire he'd received late the previous fall. He hoped to be through with the branding before this one arrived.

"Came all the way from Washington, D.C., it did," Gabe Pitts said with obvious awe. "Since I was a-headin' this way, least I could do was drop it off."

Hunter could feel Shorely's eyes on him as he looked at the postmark. Denver, February 27, 1873. It was now the twenty-fifth of March. He wouldn't finish branding now for sure. No matter . . . he would go. It was still his job, and he had Nate Gage to thank for that. No, he couldn't put all the blame on Gage. Truth was, it was hard to sever ties to a man like Gage. They had ridden through the war together and later spent years working in Washington. And now he was needed again . . . his special talent few men possessed, outside the likes of Gage himself. If it meant losing the ranch, he would still go. He owed Nate and a small, quiet man with brooding eyes that much and more.

He folded the unopened wire and stuffed it into a shirt pocket beneath his coat, noting the disappointed looks from Shorely and Pitts.

"Appreciate you bringing this out, Gabe. Set supper with us?" Gabe shook his head, wanting to move on now that he wasn't going to learn the contents of the wire.

"Got just enough light to make Beecher's camp afore dark." Thick snow engulfed them as the storm center moved over them. "Bought myself a claim yonder on the other side of them Sawatch Mountains." Whip Shorely's ears pricked up.

"'Nuther strike?" Whip asked, eyes dancing.

"Done set up a mining district. Pikers a-headed over there in droves."

Hunter sat his horse saying nothing. He hoped Whip would

12

stay; he needed him now more than ever.

Shorely rubbed his grimy beard as he studied the distant peaks that Pitts had indicated through the thick snow. Slowly he turned to look at Hunter, his beard nearly covered with the white stuff.

"Naw, reckon I'll stick, getting too long in the tooth to go traipsing around them cold mountains anymore. Besides, I got myself a real paying job." He winked at Gabe.

"Suit yourself," Gabe Pitts said.

Hunter let out a lungful of air he hadn't realized he was holding. He could feel the pressure of Nate Gage riding his shoulders already, and he touched his spurs to his horse after bidding Pitts good-bye.

One thing, storm or no, the higher draws would wait now for sure.

The spring storm blanketed the Gunnison River valley with heavy snow before moving east across the magnificent but formidable Sawatch Mountains only to die out in Tomichi Valley.

While the spring storm raged outside, Hunter settled in before the huge stone fireplace he had constructed himself while Shorely cleared away the supper dishes. He sipped at the hot coffee before placing the cup on the wide hearth in front of him. Tired but happy they had gotten as much done during the warm weather, Hunter leaned back in the chair and listened to the wind beat a familiar tune at the corner eaves. The fire felt good to his aching joints.

He fished the telegram from his pocket and broke the seal. The short sentence read:

JAMES HUNTER STOP MAKE ARRANGEMENTS
STOP ARRIVE DENVER APRIL 9 STOP
                              NATE GAGE

Short and to the point. Hunter expected nothing less from Gage. There was no need for further words. He folded the wire and returned it to his pocket.

Awhile later Shorely joined Hunter by the fire.

"You look plum give out," Shorely said, noting the tired lines around Hunter's eyes.

"Don't expect you could dance the fandango either."

"Gemme a fast lady and I'd die trying." A huge grin creased Shorely's leathery face. His eyes were bright and clear. Hunter wasn't so sure the old man wouldn't try given half the chance.

"Uh-huh. Well, don't try it. I don't feel like digging frozen ground just to get rid of your carcass." The old man roared with laughter.

"Ain't as dead as ol' Gabe." Shorely winked at Hunter. For a few minutes they shared the fire in silence, letting the day's work wash over them. Hunter was the first to break the silence.

"Whip, we got to find another hand tomorrow." Shorely looked at his boss curiously but said nothing. "I've been called to Denver on business and expect to be gone around three weeks."

"Gonna be hard findin' a good man what with everybody down with the gold fever." Hunter nodded. Since the Ute treaty, Gunnison country was flooded with miners picking and panning every stream and mountain outcropping.

"Got to try."

"This got anything to do with that wire you got today?"

"Has everything to do with it," Hunter admitted.

"Do I know this gent so all-fired important it takes you away from the most important thing in your life?"

"Could be," Hunter said casually as he got out of his chair to move across the room. Shorely watched as Hunter headed for his bedroom without another word.

"Well, you gonna leave me wonderin' all night?" Shorely asked.

"Name's Grant, Ulysses S." Hunter said softly over his shoulder. Behind him Whip Shorely let go with a low whistle.

14

CHAPTER TWO

Santa Fe Prison

The first rays of early morning glanced weakly through the barred window and gently traced a familiar path across the stone floor to touch the face of Joe Meekam. For nine years the sun had been his alarm clock. Today was different. He was awake long before the sun cleared the distant peaks. Meekam shifted to an upright position. The stone floor on his bare feet told him winter was still hanging on in New Mexico. The floor was his gauge for measuring the passing seasons. During the hot summers the stones released their stored heat of the day, making nights unbearable and sleepless, while in the winter, men shivered beneath thin blankets both night and day.

Meekam grew to tolerate the heat and the cold without complaint. In fact, he was a model prisoner, working at his duties and giving no one cause for trouble. The effort paid off. Today he was being paroled after having served nine of a fifteen-year sentence for armed robbery . . . still plenty of time to think . . . and to hate. Had they linked him with Jim Reynolds, Meekam knew he would have been hanged instead.

Around him Meekam heard the familiar sounds of the prison coming to life. He stood to pull on his pants. In the distance guard doors opened and closed with a metallic ring. He turned to pack his few belongings. One change of clothes, a straight razor he was finally given the luxury of owning, a cigar box of odds and ends, and a weathered photograph of a smiling-faced boy in what looked to be a new suit of ill-fitting clothes. Meekam studied the face of his kid brother, Billy, for a long moment before putting it into his coat pocket.

The face of his kid brother and a place called Shiloh burned in his brain like a chronic fever—for more than ten years. The hate for Benton and Grant ate at him like acid. Meekam smiled coldly to himself as he made ready to leave the cell. Only recently did he learn Benton had been shot by a deserter. It seemed fitting an end to a man who sent a lot of good men to their graves because of the power given to him by General Grant.

Meekam wished he had been the one to pull the trigger. No matter, Grant gave the orders and Meekam's singular hate for this man carried him through the last ten years. It was his only reason for living. And now Grant was coming to Colorado. Things were finally shifting his way for a change . . . and about time. His cell door clanked open.

"Well, Meekam, you packed and ready?" Tom Miller asked. A guard for nearly twenty years, Miller could usually size up a new prisoner in a matter of days, yet this quiet man with the brooding eyes remained unfathomable. There was one thing Miller was sure of though—Meekam was a volcano ready to explode.

Meekam looked at the guard, his face expressionless. "Been ready," he said as a way of greeting and saying good-bye.

"Bet you have." Meekam stepped lightly from the cell without a backward glance. Silent-eyed men watched from a double row of cells as Meekam and the guard passed. The prison was strangely quiet for someone getting out. Meekam couldn't care less. A loner, Meekam was leaving no friends behind. He knew he would never return. What he had planned, he doubted he would live past that moment. It mattered little to him, for he had already died with his brother a long time ago.

Two trail-weary riders with the Texas stamp hunkered in the cold, dusty street across from the prison. They had ridden in earlier, leading a gray-flecked stallion. One was a burly man with deep red hair and beard. He passed his time drawing in the dirt street with a stick. The other man was short with an open, friendly face who contented himself with chewing a strip of jerky, ignoring the bigger man's scribblings.

Awhile later, a tall, ramrod-straight figure emerged from the prison and crossed the street to where the Texans waited. The three men shook hands. A minute later the Texans and the man now riding the stallion cleared the dusty street of Santa Fe at a fast clip, heading north toward the distant snowy peaks of the Sangre de Cristo Mountains.

CHAPTER THREE

Jim Hunter bent over to look closely in the fast-fading light at the slack face and vacant eyes of the man who had, just moments before, tried to kill him. He didn't recognize the dead man with the flaming red hair and beard.

Straightening, Hunter looked around the cold landscape, searching for signs of further danger. The canyon was covered with a foot of late spring snow. They were alone as far as he could determine. He eased the hammer down on his carbine while examining the hole where the stranger's bullet had burned the upper left sleeve of his coat. Had he not shifted in the saddle to ease a cramped back, Hunter felt sure the .44/40 slug would have found its mark. A cold sweat broke out between his shoulder blades at the thought.

He searched the dead man's pockets, finding nothing more than a few dollars and a supply list. Next he searched the rocks higher in the canyon for the man's horse. Hunter found the big sorrel tied in a clump of aspen and spruce. Upon his back was an orante silver-trimmed saddle some riders along the Texas-Mexico border favored. A search of the saddlebags and bedroll revealed nothing further about the man. A case of mistaken identity? Maybe an old enemy out to even a score? Hardly. As far as Hunter was aware, no one back east knew where he was outside of Gage and a few close friends. Unconsciously he found himself touching the pocket where he kept the telegram. Had it something to do with the President? This worried him even more. Hunter untied the big horse and led him down the rocky slope to where the dead man lay.

Hunter spoke softly to the sorrel as the animal shied away from the prostrate figure of his master, his nostrils flaring wide.

18

The wind sprang up over the high ridge above Hunter as a gentle breeze at first, then quickly grew into a fury. The jagged peaks ripped holes in the thin undersides of the low-moving clouds, dumping wet snow into the canyon.

Swiftly Hunter tore the gun belt from the dead man and retrieved his rifle a few feet from where the man had dropped it after taking his only shot, square in the chest. The snow was coming down hard now, and within minutes the death scene would be completely obliterated. Suddenly Hunter saw it, half covered with the new snow and but a few feet from where he picked up the man's rifle. Hunter studied the fully extended spyglass for a moment. A strange chill shot through him. The man obviously knew who he was shooting at all along. One thing was certain, he could rule out robbery.

After one last look at the dead man, Hunter moved upslope a half mile with the horses and made camp in a jumble of boulders in a small draw intermixed with a few scraggly spruce and pine. It offered some protection from the chilling winds and blowing snow. He stripped the gear from both horses and set about making camp, his mind busy with the dead man below. Later as he lay in his blankets beneath a lean-to, he let his thoughts drift back through a list of familiar faces trying to pick out the big red-haired man. He came up blank. It wasn't like him to forget a face. He couldn't afford to—his livelihood depended on it. A vague uneasiness settled over him, and he felt as if he gripped the end of a huge ball of string that could unwind at any moment and in any direction. He didn't like feeling helpless. The thought irritated him deeply and he put it aside. He thought of the ranch and wondered how Whip was making out with the hastily hired hand. It had been hard to find anyone willing to work cattle with Gunnison valley crawling with gold-fevered miners. He only hoped the kid would stay long enough to get most of the cattle out of the higher draws and canyons before the fever hit him again. Nothing he could do about it now as he cleared his head for sleep. The wind was nothing more than a low moan through the trees, and the falling snow whispered against the tarpaulin as Hunter drifted into a watchful sleep.

Just before dawn, during that period when night is blackest,

Hunter came instantly awake. Something or someone was out there. Unmoving, he lay in his blankets, listening for further sounds. It had stopped snowing and the wind was nothing more than a gentle sigh. The fire had long since been covered with snow. The only light was reflected from the overhead stars shining through the broken cloud cover. Then he heard it. A muffled noise, like clothing being brushed against a tree. Slowly Hunter slipped his revolver from beneath the covers. Swiftly he stepped clear of his lean-to and stood with his back against the boulder he had used to shield his fire. He scanned the night for signs of the intruder. Lighting was poor at best, and he could see only a few feet in any direction.

His mind was filled with the possibility the dead man below had something to do with this when he smelled the horrible breath of the grizzly at his back. Instinctively he spun around crouching for safety as the giant bear descended upon him. Desperately Hunter brought the heavy .44 Colt up to fire. So close was the bear that the barrel tip was buried in the huge beast's thick fur. It was the only shot Hunter got off, striking the animal in its neck. The muffled noise of the gun was drowned out by the thunderous roar that rose up from the grizzly's throat as he crushed Hunter to him. For a moment Hunter thought he would pass out, and then suddenly he was no longer part of what was happening. As if from a distance, he saw the huge jaws of the monster descend upon his head, ripping the scalp to the bone. Next the bloody mouth locked on a shoulder and lifted him high overhead. He continued to look on the scene but felt no pain. The bear shook him savagely before tossing him several yards away, where he landed in a heap, unmoving. The wounded bear seemed to go crazy, as if finally realizing the heavy slug had caused major damage. He gave Hunter a powerful swat. Hunter did not move.

In a blind rage the bear made shambles of the camp. The horses had long since been spooked off by the bear's presence. Every so often the grizzly would return to Hunter and give him a swipe. Growling his satisfaction that the thing who had hurt him was dead, he went back to destroying the camp. This continued for nearly an hour. It was one of the bear's swipes that laid Hunter's rib cage open and brought him back to consciousness.

Hunter lay in shock, looking up through the blood and pain at the cold points of lights overhead as they began to fade with the pink glow from the east. He stifled a cry building deep within his wounded body. The huge bear still rumbled around the damaged camp. Hunter was drenched in the sticky wetness of his own blood as well as being light-headed from the loss. He heard the bear coming back again, and he realized with a start he still clutched his six-gun. Miraculously he had instinctively hung on to the weapon throughout the bear's onslaught. It took all his remaining strength to bring the hammer back to full cock. He fought back the blackness building behind his eyes. Suddenly he heard the ragged breathing of the grizzly at his side.

Hunter took a deep painful breath and allowed his instincts to take charge. Just as the beast came into his line of vision, he lifted the Colt and fired instantly without aiming, something years of training and experience had taught him. In that same instant, blackness swept over him.

CHAPTER FOUR

The smell of wood smoke and coffee stirred Hunter's senses, and the darkness lifted. He swallowed hard, his throat aching from the effort, and slowly he opened his eyes. A burly, heavily whiskered man dressed in greasy, rough leathers was bending over a campfire. His reddish beard was heavily laced with streaks of gray. Without looking up, the man spoke. The lingo of a trapper or mountain man.

"Been wonderin' when you wuz comin' 'round. Course, I allowed you been put to the test with that griz."

Hunter tried to speak, but the words stuck in his parched throat. He coughed, and the effort sent a knifelike wave of pain through his chest, causing him to cry out. The man by the fire looked at Hunter for the first time, his eyes the color of the overhead sky.

"Wouldn't move 'round much if'n I wuz you. You might break open an' go to bleedin'. Best you lay still if you can. Got just the ticket to make you feel like livin' again. You look a mite feverish too."

Hunter lay waiting for the pain to subside. He watched the big man fill a bowl from a bubbling pot. Hunter used the time to survey the camp. His horse was busily nibbling at the swollen buds of the aspen he was tied to. He didn't see the big sorrel. His eyes caught the large dull brown area where he had fought the grizzly. The man strode over and knelt by Hunter.

"Try this on, son. Ain't nobody in these here parts makes a better stew," he said with obvious pride. He smelled of bear grease and smoke from a thousand campfires.

Hunter ate the thick rich stew as the trapper looked on, pleased. He fetched them both a cup of coffee and hunkered down by Hunter.

"That was really good. Didn't know I was so hungry. I'm grateful." Hunter accepted the strong coffee from the mountain man. "I'm James Hunter," he said, offering his hand.

"Henry Sawtelle," the man replied, covering Hunter's hand with a huge, steely fist. "Most folks jest call me Buck fer short." Hunter sipped at the hot liquid and burned his tongue.

"Guess ya wonderin' how I come to find you and the griz a huggin' one another yestiddy morning?" Buck ventured.

"I've been out that long?"

"Heered yore shot. Wuz dry-camped farther up this here ridge a-huntin' fer elk. I'd a been to home if'n the storm had'na hit when it did. Lucky fer you these old eyes ain't what they once wuz." Buck looked off, scanning the ridge for signs of life with a practiced eye.

"Don't get me wrong. I can still see as good as ever outen front of me. But it wuz close to night and the snow wuz flyin' thick as bees. Lordy, but Jay must be a-thinkin' I done walked ofen one of them outcroppings."

"Jay?"

"My daughter. But the way she carries on, you'd a think she wuz my mother," Buck said with a twinkle in his eye.

Hunter smiled, and a sharp pain shot across his face, bringing tears to his eyes. Sawtelle saw the pain reflected in Hunter's expression.

"You got a couple a bad cuts along the ridge of yore jaw," he said sympathetically. "Done the best I could with what wuz left of you."

"Owe you my life . . . and I won't forget it."

"Aww, I'd a done the same fer any man," Buck replied, "even fer a low-down Blackfoot er Digger Injun, knowing I might hafta kill him later." Hunter had no doubt the trapper meant it.

"Anyways, I come on yore camp, er what wuz left of it, and seed that griz stretched outen on the ground. Didn't know you wuz underneath till later. Whiter'n the snow, you wuz . . . 'cept fer the blood, a course."

"I was under the bear?" Hunter asked, not believing his ears.

Buck chuckled. "Fer a fact. Figgered you fer dead. Griz kept you from freezin' to death. Skinned her out and jerked most the meat except fer the stew and what's a-hangin' in that spruce. Hunter eased down again, weak as branch water. He shivered from the cold and pulled the blankets up to his chin. Buck covered him with the bear hide.

"That oughta warm you up a mite," he said, and he went back to the fire. "Never did find yore pack animal," he added casually as he lit his pipe from a burning twig. "Guess he hightailed it outa here when the griz attacked you?"

"Pack animal?" And then Hunter understood the oblique question. The dead man's saddle was in plain view. One man didn't ride two saddles. Before he could explain, he saw Buck's face change to one of wariness.

"We got company."

CHAPTER FIVE

Hunter came instantly alert. His first thoughts were of his gun and that whoever was out there was connected to the dead man in the canyon. Buck let go a huge plume of blue smoke that surrounded his head for a moment then trailed lazily upward into the thin blue sky. He drifted casually over to his bedroll to where his rifle lay. Other than a large knife at his belt, he carried no other weapons.

"They's two of them," Buck said, "about three hundred yards out. Near hid by that large outcroppin' of rocks and spruce jest to the north of where you lay." Hunter let his eyes scan the area below the ridge line until he found them sitting their horses, unmoving.

"If yore feelin' sorta naked, I put yore gun 'neath the covers with you," Buck said, acting unconcerned at the two men's presence. "Figgered any man kept his gun and holster as well oiled—" He caught himself. "What I mean is—" Hunter cut him off.

"I understand." He found the gun as Buck promised and did take comfort in it being near. In his condition he wasn't sure how much good it would do.

"Guess they scouted us long enough to figger they held the edge on an old man and a cripple," Buck said lightly, yet his face was one of serious study as the two men walked their horses slowly down the slope. They pulled up twenty-five yards out, and their eyes darted about the camp.

The taller of the two held a rifle across his saddle. Sitting his horse straight like some general, the man's face was chisel hard, and he stared out from beneath the brim of his hat with pale gray eyes. He sported a large drooping mustache beneath an aquiline nose, and his mouth was set in a flat line. His close-set eyes found Hunter's and lingered a moment. Hunter felt as if he had looked a snake in the eye at close range. This one, with his flat, expressionless gaze, was dangerous, and Hunter would have to be careful. Hunter looked at the other man. He was short and stocky and had a casual air of slouchness about him. With an open face and friendly eyes, the man had none of the hardness found in his riding companion. For a fleeting moment Hunter had the strange feeling he knew the man. He noted their lingering looks at the silver-trimmed saddle and he silently cursed himself for not having taken better precaution.

The tall one leaned forward slightly and shot a brown stream into a patch of snow, his face thrust forward belligerently as if daring the two to make a hostile move.

"Something we can do fer you gents?" Buck Sawtelle asked, breaking the silence. The tone of the question was neither friendly nor antagonistic, more like the quiet acceptance of whatever was to come. Hunter calculated the old mountain man had faced greater adversaries in his time.

The tall one turned his head slightly in Buck's direction but kept Hunter in his peripheral vision. When he spoke he acted as if it pained him to answer the old man.

"Looking for someone," he said with a soft southern drawl, yet sounded like dry gravel beneath one's feet.

"That a fact," Buck replied with mock seriousness. "And who might that be?" The man's eyes slid to Hunter and back again to Buck.

"What happened to *him?*" he said, ignoring Buck's question. It riled Hunter that he was not asked directly, yet he curbed his tongue. The old trapper was a picture of calmness.

"Tangled with a griz," Buck responded. "Griz lost." The man merely grunted, as if to say the grizzly had not lost by much. Hunter could feel his anger building, but he didn't want to start anything that would involve Buck in his affairs. He knew who they were searching for and he could feel the ball of string starting to unwind. The short one spoke as if to ease the building tension.

"As Joe was saying, we are looking for my . . . ah, a friend. He's a day overdue." Joe glared hard at his companion, clearly not pleased over the use of his name or for having butted in on the conversation. Hunter instinctively tightened his grip on his revolver.

"Big redheaded fellow. Goes by Toby," Joe said. "Sets a saddle like the fancy one over there." Hunter could feel the open challenge in the man's voice. The ball of string was really rolling now. Buck was standing free and easy, ready to kick the fracas off if necessary.

"No law against having two saddles," Hunter replied, wanting to draw as much information from the two as he could. Joe's eyes raked Hunter with impunity, as if looking at a squashed bug under his boot.

"We got yore drift," Buck interjected, cutting off any reply the two men might have made. "Suppose you haul yore carcasses outen here, *now!*" Miraculously Buck was standing there holding the old buffalo gun lazily in his huge hands, and it was aimed at the pit of Joe's stomach. The two men were as surprised as Hunter.

Joe's face went flat, and he glared hard at the trapper, knowing he no longer held the advantage. A gun like the old coot was holding could blow a hole in you large enough to trail a herd through.

Hunter mustered the strength to raise himself to a sitting position. He left his hand with the revolver beneath the cover. He had never let anyone do his fighting for him, and he wasn't about to start now. His voice was granite hard when he spoke.

"Hold it! This has gone far enough. The man you are looking for lies back in the canyon a ways . . . dead. Tried to dry-gulch me." The short one's face turned white and then a dusty red.

"You're lying!" he shouted. Joe put an arm out to restrain the other man, his face like chiseled stone.

"I've told you the straight of it," Hunter said with a hard edge. "Why did he try to kill me?"

"We'll have ourselves a look at who's below. If it is Toby, then, mister, this ain't noway settled." Abruptly he wheeled his horse around and pounded back in the direction he had come with his companion glaring back at Hunter.

Hunter sank back to the ground and closed his eyes, spent for the moment. He was chilled to the bone.

"Reckon we ain't seed the last a them critters," Buck said as he laid the rifle on his bedroll. He glanced over at Hunter. Hafta get him back to the cabin and quick, Buck thought. He needed the care only Jay could give now. Buck had cared for a lot of sick people in his time and he knew Hunter would be damn lucky if he survived the ride to the cabin. Hunter's face was cherry red as he dropped into a troubled sleep.

Buck packed the camp. Only five or six miles from the cabin, he figured. Not an easy ride for a man in Hunter's condition, Buck knew, but he had no choice. Jay was his best bet.

He cast a practiced eye skyward as he finished packing. The bright sky belied the storm Buck knew was building to the west of the high ridge. A biting wind had risen sharply. In high mountain passes springtime could be as rough and unpredictable as any winter weather. It was either going to sleet or snow like hell, or both. He glanced over at Hunter and speeded up the packing.

They climbed the high ridge, putting the trees and rocks between themselves and the camp below. Finally Joe Meekam jerked his horse to a savage stop. Quirt Tyler, trailing close behind, almost rode him down. The ride upward had been punishing for the flatlander horses, and they stood with their sides heaving.

"What in hell got into Toby?" Meekam spit out, his hard eyes on Quirt. Quirt had been thinking the same thing.

"Dunno, but I aim to make that jasper pay. That was Toby's saddle he fancied so much." Frankly Quirt never could understand what possessed Toby to buy it. Too gaudy for him. But Toby had never been right after he was thrown into a pile of rocks by a raw-broke mustang when the war was over. And now Toby was dead. For some reason the face of his brother's killer kept nagging at him.

Meekam shook his head at how things were going. "If I had known how bad off Toby was, I would never have sent for you two."

"He couldn't help it," Quirt said, rising to defend his dead brother. "Them rocks busted something loose inside his head."

"Even so, Toby brought it on himself. Let's get one thing straight before we continue. Nothing, and I do mean nothing, is going to interfere with my plans. You want to cut loose, now is the time. I'll understand . . . but you ride out *now*. No coming back." Quirt looked at Meekam's hard face and he knew he meant every word.

"I'm staying," he said quietly, "but I want to give Toby a decent burial."

"Fair enough. Make camp and tend to it first thing tomorrow." They rode on through the rocky country with Quirt questioning his sanity for staying. He could have cut a trail to Texas, but deep down he knew the reason for his staying did not involve his brother. Gold, pure and simple. They were after gold, like Toby had whispered to him on their way west to join Meekam. It meant gunplay at some point, but Quirt was ready for that too. A two-bit cattle rustler who ran a few head south into Mexico when he got the chance, Quirt knew if he was ever going to get away from his pa and that dirt farm, this riding with Meekam would be it. Not even Toby or his pa knew about his operation, cut short after Toby rode in late one night from Colorado after the Reynolds gang had been busted up by the law. Joe Meekam had been caught and Toby was afraid they were after him, so he and Toby left early that morning to join the war. Meekam interrupted his thoughts.

"We'll make camp in that hollow among those rocks. Rough weather tonight, 'less I miss my guess." Quirt looked at the clear sky, wondering how Meekam knew this. He hated being up this high. Chilled to the bone, he kept a constant headache. Almost wished he had stayed in Texas. At least a man wouldn't freeze to death this time of year.

CHAPTER SIX

As Buck predicted, the storm swept across the rugged mountains with full fury late in the day bringing heavy waves of sleet mixed with big flakes of wet snow.

Hunter, delirious with fever, slumped forward over the neck of his horse, too weak to do otherwise. He moaned under his breath as Buck gently tied him to the saddle and draped the big bearskin over him and lashed it down.

The sky darkened as if nighttime had settled in prematurely, only to be lit every few seconds by bolts of brilliant blue-white lightning. Thunder reverberated across the rocky peaks and high canyon walls.

The trip to the cabin was long and treacherous in the blinding storm. The trail, such as it was, cut through high mountain meadows, across rushing streams swollen by the storm, and through tall stands of pine and spruce. Parts of the trail were sharp switchbacks across loose talus. Over these areas Buck gave his horse his head, letting him pick his way across the slippery rocks. As they climbed higher the sleet turned to snow.

Buck pointed his horse into the bitter cold wind, pulling his hat lower on his head. Occasionally he glanced back at the ice-covered lump that was Hunter.

To Hunter, the trip was a kaleidoscope of white flashes, thunder, and pleasant dreams of people and places long forgotten. In moments of rational thought, he looked out from his bear cave at the broad back of the trapper, knowing his survival depended totally on him.

Hunter felt himself being moved, yet there was no pain. Voices and strong hands worked over him, and the smell of lilac mixed with the odor of cooked food drifted through the fevered fog that gripped his mind and body like a vise. The urge to give in to the blackness was overwhelming. He heard a female voice say something, yet the words were scrambled and indecipherable. The voice and soft hands were comforting, and slowly he gave in to the thick mist.

Buck stuck his head around the thin curtain acting as a room divider. He held a mug of black coffee laced with a little whiskey.

"How's he doing, Jay?" She had insisted on placing Hunter in her bed which was softer and a little more private. Buck learned long ago never to argue with a woman. Only critters on the earth he had failed to figure out, and it didn't matter if they were Shoshone, Mexican, or white, they all possessed the same unfathomable quality. But he had done his share of trying over the years.

Janett looked up at her father's heavily seamed brown face. She finished changing the bloody makeshift bandages Buck used on Hunter. The air hung heavy with the sharp smell of spirits.

"I don't see how he is still alive," she remarked, gathering up the soiled bandages along with Hunter's clothes. "He barely has a pulse, and his fever is dangerously high." Jay brushed past Buck with the bundle.

Buck turned back to the warmth of the fireplace. "Reckon if anybody can pull him through, you can." Jay looked at her father benignly.

"I'm not a doctor, so don't expect miracles. Remember, I only assisted Dr. Lancaster."

"Hell, same difference out here," Buck snorted. "You ain't in St. Louis no more, child. And what we got outen here this side a Denver don't begin to measure up to what you done back east."

Jay smiled to herself as she heated food for Buck. She admitted, things were really different here. She had no idea how much until she talked Buck into letting her come back with him after her mother's funeral. He kept telling her the mountains were no place for a lady, yet eight months had passed and she couldn't be happier.

As a wild-eyed kid she used to dream of the distant places Buck told her about on his trips back to St. Louis. After her mother's death, she had nothing to prevent her from seeing this wild country firsthand and learn what strange hold the place had on her father. Most of all, she wanted to get to know Buck before it was too late.

Buck settled himself by the fire while howling winds piled two feet of new snow around the snug cabin. He packed the bowl of his pipe while studying his daughter. At thirty, she was the very essence of her mother. Her long black hair fell in beautiful waves around a face that held wide-set eyes the color of an alpine spruce, high cheekbones softened by a properly centered nose that flared delicately at the tip. Buck sighed deeply, settling back in his chair as the fire warmed up his aching joints. He was listening dreamily to the storm outside, recalling another time and another woman with long black hair, when Jay called him to supper.

Meanwhile, a half-dozen rugged miles away, two men huddled beneath a tarp staring into the flames of a small campfire. They had not spoken much in the last hour. Quirt pulled the thin Texas blanket closer around him, shivering inwardly. Christ, he had never been so cold. He stole a look at the grim-faced Meekam, wondering what was eating him.

"What now?" Quirt asked more to break the silence than to answer a real need to know. Meekam stared silently at the Texan as if considering the question. Actually he had been determining the true worth of the man to him now.

"Why didn't you go into Fairplay for supplies like I asked?"

"Toby wanted to go. Wanted to see if any of his old friends were still around," Quirt said defensively.

"Friends!" Meekam snarled. "Outside of us, Toby had no friends." Quirt seemed to shrink under Meekam's attack. How he let himself become saddled with a couple of lightweights Meekam would never know. He rubbed his jaw thoughtfully.

"Tomorrow you get what few supplies we need and a newspaper if you can find one. I'll keep looking for the canyon." Meekam had spent three days searching for the canyon without success, which did nothing to improve his disposition. Ten years made a big difference, plus the night of the running gun battle with the posse hadn't given him much time to mark the place where he had hidden the gold. He thought about that night for the thousandth time, hoping to remember something new about the canyon. He and the Reynolds gang hit the Buckskin Joe stage at McLaughlin's station just east of Fairplay. A determined posse scattered the gang but not before Meekam stuffed his saddlebags with gold bullion. Riding for miles in the pitch blackness, a lone lawman clung to Meekam's trail. Topping a high ridge, Meekam stopped on the downslope side to cache the gold. The added weight was killing his horse and he needed the horse more than the gold. He saw a light in a cabin far below him as he piled loose rock over the saddlebags at the base of a huge, leaning ponderosa. Afterward he lost the lawman and joined Toby for a hard ride to the south.

Not much to go on now, he admitted to himself. One good thing: No one, not even Reynolds or Toby, knew he had buried any gold. It was still there, waiting for him now.

"You think you can find the canyon?" Quirt asked, wanting to steer the subject clear of Toby.

"I can find it," Meekam answered flatly, "if this damn snow lets up any."

Quirt Tyler hesitated, unsure of how to broach the subject now that his brother was dead. The loss was something tangible, and he wondered how Meekam had dealt with his own brother's death.

"Joe," Tyler spoke softly, "what happened at Shiloh? I mean, me and Toby never did know how Billy died . . . only that he died." For a moment Meekam looked at the Texan with the cold eyes of death, and his first impulse was to strike out at Tyler for jarring painful memories. Maybe it was because Tyler had just buried a brother, a simple act, yet something Meekam was denied under the circumstances of war, for which he would forever be bitter. Or was it the simple need to share the hurt he carried so deeply inside? In truth, Meekam didn't know . . . or really care that much. Billy was gone, and no amount of talking was going to bring him back. How could he describe the cold anger that was with him every waking minute?

Meekam looked past the lean-to at the white gloom and began talking, slowly at first, and then all the pent-up words rushed out of him in a steady stream.

"We were part of Peacock's troops. Had us out before dawn. It was pitch black and no one knew why we were being forced to leave behind our field gear. Figured it out later, after lying in the bushes with a bullet in my leg. We were sent out only to locate Johnny Reb's position and report back. I can still smell the stench of the place—the mud, the blood. For three days it rained and everything and everyone was wet to the bone. Sleep was impossible." Meekam reached out and shoved the coffeepot deeper into the ashes. "Worried more about Billy dying of pneumonia than a Confederate bullet. Anyway, we found Rebs all right, but it wasn't no sentry post. Wasn't long we were in a pitch battle with a major troop movement. They pushed us back so hard and fast we had to run just to stay alive. The place was smoking with Rebs like a bunch of yellow jackets out of the ground. Billy and me managed to drop back to a shallow slough while the main force pushed our men clear back to Owl Creek. That's when I caught a bullet in the thigh. Wasn't for Billy, I would have died right there." Without thinking, Meekam added fresh snow to the pot. Tyler could see the pain etched in his face. "Billy managed to hide me in a thicket near the Tennessee. Hell, we could look down from the bluff and see Grant's steamer tied up at Pittsburg Landing. The wood hung heavy with smoke and screams of the dying on both sides. Rebs had our troops running around like a bunch of pissants at a Sunday picnic. We were well hidden, so we didn't worry too much about being spotted. I dozed off and on all afternoon while the fighting continued. Remember being real thirsty, probably 'cause I lost so much blood. Got Peacock to thank for that. None of us were given time for breakfast. Guess Peacock figured to be back before the coffee got hot," Meekam said with grim humor. "Somebody forgot to tell the Rebs."

"Shouda been wearing the Gray all along," Quirt blurted out. Meekam looked at Tyler with burning eyes.

"Blame Paw for that. Billy and me should have run off from him once we got to Pennsylvania. All we wanted was to stay in the Del Norte Mountains even though Paw wasn't making a go of the farm. One thing I regret—we waited too long to desert the army. Kept waiting to get closer to Texas . . . cost Billy his life."

"You didn't know."

"Maybe so, but if we had cut out earlier, Billy would be here now. Benton caught Billy out in the open taking a knapsack from a dead Union soldier."

"Benton?"

"Worked for Grant. His job was to round up deserters. Instead, he and his men usually just shot them on the spot. The way they did Billy. They cut him down without a word. Billy jerked—" Meekam stopped talking and looked out into the night. His guts felt on fire. "Never thought I'd tell that to anyone."

"Knew something bad had happened when you rode through and Toby left with you for Colorado."

A sneer crossed Meekam's face. "We were supposed to steal smelted gold for the Confederate cause. Jack Reynolds was like we were, out for what we could get for ourselves. Had enough fighting and dying for a cause . . . North or South. Quantrill was doing the same only he was better known." Silence fell for a long moment between the pair at the fire while soft winds eased through the spruce trees with a gentle sigh.

Quirt Tyler realized few people had ever seen beneath Meekam's tough exterior as he just had. What softness was there was well hidden, and a man would be a fool to count on Meekam for mercy. The outlaw cared for no one or anything anymore, and Tyler knew it.

"We find the gold, what then?" Tyler asked. Meekam was pouring coffee and he held the pot in midair for a moment. It was a fair question. A man ought to know what's expected of him when it meant almost certain death. He finished pouring the coffee, handed it to Quirt, and filled a cup for himself.

"We'll head to Denver. Hire a few good men." The wind changed direction suddenly and thick snow swirled around the two men.

"There is one thing," Meekam said, looking down at the offending flakes settling in his cup, his eyes suddenly hard again. "You tell anyone of my plans before I'm ready, I'll kill you."

Quirt blinked as he looked into Meekam's hooded eyes. He could only shake his head mutely.

And as another gust of snow whipped around the two men, Meekam's next words turned Quirt to stone.

CHAPTER SEVEN

The day broke bright and clear. The sun cast a brilliance across the pristine snow and every sound seemed magnified in the sharp, cold air. Buck had been out tending to the horses, and as he entered the cabin with an armload of wood, he heard voices. The whole cabin shook when he dumped the load next to the fire.

The thundering noise sent Hunter to a bolt-upright position in bed. Jay was feeding him a hot clear broth. She laughed at the stricken look on his face.

"That's just Buck," Jay said as a way of explanation. "Thinks he has to carry a cord in at a time." Hunter smiled weakly.

"How ya feelin', son?" Buck roared from the other side of the curtain.

"He also doesn't know when he is inside," she added ruefully as her father stuck his head around the curtain. His eyes fairly sparkled. Buck noted Hunter's dull eyes and pale complexion. He was a long way from being out of the woods yet.

"She feedin' ya that stuff. May as well give up and die," Buck said solemnly. "Took the fever once. Fool child poured enough that stuff down my gullet to fill the crick. It was two months afore I needed a drink a water. Durn near kilt me."

"Never mind what Buck says. He was mad only because I made him stay in bed longer than six hours at a time." Hunter could see for all their bantering, they were very close.

"It's really good," Hunter insisted, taking another spoonful to prove it. "I feel better already."

"Wal, if you live till night, I'll fix a steak offin' that griz you kilt. Then you will feel fit." He said to Jay, "Fever gone?"

36

"Peaked at three and was gone by five this morning." She looked tired and her eyes showed it.

"You been up all night with me?"

"Had to bathe you with alcohol to keep the fever down," she said simply.

"Go pile on my bed, child, and get some sleep," Buck said tenderly.

"I've taken your bed as well?" Hunter moved as if to get up.

"Stay where you are," Jay said firmly. "You want to start bleeding again?" Hunter protested but allowed himself to be recovered.

"Better listen to her, son. She's been at this nursin' game fer a spell."

Hunter looked at Jay. "A nurse?"

"Back in St. Louis."

"Go on, girl, get some sleep now," Buck prodded. "Need to talk with this here pilgrim." Hunter put his hand on her arm as she stood to leave. She looked down into his gold-flecked eyes.

"Want to thank you . . . for saving my life. I won't forget it."

She colored under his open stare. "I'm glad you are going to be okay," she said simply. Hunter dropped his hand, and she disappeared around the curtain. Buck pulled the straight chair closer to the bed and eased his big frame down heavily.

"Smoke?" Buck asked, putting a match to his pipe.

"Never acquired the habit."

"That's almighty upstandin'," Buck reflected. "Got into the habit from all them peace-pipe days with the Sioux, Pawnee, and such." Buck leaned forward and whispered conspiratorially, "Weren't the only thang I learned from them Injuns." Hunter smiled, and pain raced across his jaw.

"Had myself a look-see where you kilt that fellar when I went back fer the rest of the griz. Body wuz gone but they wuz two sets a tracks rode in and when they rode out, one set wuz a lot deeper." Buck read sign like Hunter could read a newspaper. "Guess they found Toby," Buck said dryly.

"I spoke the truth," Hunter said. "About how I killed him."

"Never figgered no different, son."

"Buck, what day is this? I've lost all track of time."

37

"March thirtieth, and spring is on the wind."

"I must be in Denver by the ninth of April."

Buck pulled on his pipe, studying Hunter. "Ain't shore you gonna be fit fer sech a long ride. Course you could allus take the stage outen Fairplay. Runs three times a week and it only takes eighteen hours." The broth and the warm cabin made Hunter's eyes heavy-lidded and he had trouble staying awake. He still had plenty of time to get there, he calculated. Stage would be fine.

Hunter's thoughts floated free of his grip, and he felt Jay's warm hands over him again, only to be replaced by the hard-piercing eyes of Nate Gage. His eyes flew open. Nate seemed so real. Buck's chair was empty, yet the fragrance of his pipe lingered. He closed his eyes again, drifting into a peaceful sleep devoid of images.

At that moment Nate Gage, special assistant in charge of security and personal bodyguard for the President of the United States, snapped the gold lid shut on his pocket watch. Thirty minutes late. Damn! In addition to his regular duties, Gage was also the official timekeeper. The more off schedule things became, the more irritable and jumpy Gage got. It allowed for slack time, and slack time usually spelled trouble. And he didn't like surprises.

Nate scowled up the tracks at the train engineer, propped lazily against a huge wheel, talking with his brakeman. His anger began to rise. "Who the hell did they think they had on this train?" he muttered.

He started up the track at a fast clip, pulling his coat aside to hook his thumbs in his vest pockets. The act allowed the walnut butt of the Starr Army .44 to protrude openly. Nate preferred the shorter-barreled double-action gun for close quarters. For emergencies he also carried a fifty-caliber boot pistol. Dressed in fine black broadcloth and matching flat-brimmed hat, Nate Gage stood four inches over six feet and cut an impressive figure.

The train engineer saw him approaching out of the corner of his eye. He already knew who Nate was, and he was somewhat awed and a little frightened of the big man. He broke off further conversation with the brakeman as Nate strode up, his big boots kicking gravel in their direction.

"Pleasant day, isn't it?" Nate said casually. A light smile touched the corners of his mouth, yet not the hawkish eyes. The engineer coughed self-consciously, removing his hat to wipe the sweat from his forehead. Suddenly the day had become uncomfortably warm. He looked up at the imposing figure and back again to the hat he was turning nervously in his hands, not knowing what to say. The brakeman moved off to study the train wheels as if seeing them for the first time.

"What seems to be the problem?" Nate Gage asked, still in a pleasant tone.

"You see, Mr. Gage, we had a slight problem taking on water, but everything's fine now. Should be up to steam in another ten minutes."

Nate's eyes bored into the engineer. "Then you have forty minutes to make up," he said flatly, his voice losing all trace of gentleness.

The engineer shifted from one foot to the other. He could have sworn the big man's eyes changed from a rust-flecked gray to a dark steel dust while he was looking at them.

"I was told the President liked to sort a ease along so's he could enjoy the countryside."

"Correct you are, Mr. . . . ?"

"Uh, Hawkins, sir, Bill Hawkins," the engineer stammered.

"Well then, Mr. Hawkins, when you make up the forty minutes," Gage said, even-voiced, "you can rock along easy like." He paused for effect. "Until then you push this bastard for all it's worth. Understood!" Wheeling about without waiting for Hawkins to reply, Gage stalked back down the track.

"Jeezus," Hawkins whispered. He felt as relieved as a bug who had just barely missed getting stepped on. He turned to the brakeman.

"You heard the man, Frank. Get your ass up there and help the tallow pot out," Hawkins said, referring to the fireman. "I want that firebox cherry red and the pressure ready to bust the jacket when I let her roll."

Frank Hamblen hastily complied with Hawkins's orders even though he could have refused such a lowly task. But he wanted his own locomotive someday, and on board with the President was the Union Pacific's vice president, Thomas C. Durant; Sidney Dillion, the U.P. director; but more important to Hamblen, the chief engineer, Grenville Dodge. Without blessings from Dodge, Hamblen would never ride in the four-dollar seat. It wasn't just the pay, he was already at three dollars a day, but more the privilege of having his own locomotive. Could even put his name on the side of the cab. To Hamblen that was living in grand style.

Minutes later, Hawkins climbed into the cab, feeling the quiet rumble of the locomotive's giant heartbeat beneath his feet. He knew without so much as a glance at the pressure gauge that she was up to steam. He let go two sharp blasts of his whistle to alert the conductor of the train's imminent departure.

"All right, boys," Hawkins said to the laboring men covered with sweat, "old fifty-six is gonna show them city slickers just how fast a Matthias Baldwin can go when she's a mind to." He checked the track to see if it was clear. The metal thump under him was pumping harder now, as if anticipating the engineer's next move. Hawkins pushed the brake forward and opened the throttle gently at first until the ol' girl got her running legs beneath her and then gradually increased the speed. At each position the metal heartbeat of the engine matched the throttle's.

CHAPTER EIGHT

The next few days were a blur for Hunter. Everything seemed disjointed and out of focus. He slept not knowing whether it was day or night. On the fifth day, he woke clearheaded in the late afternoon to the smell of frying meat. A sharp hunger pain shot through his stomach. He was ravenous. Gingerly he brought himself to a sitting position, aware of every movement. Hunter felt as if he had been bronc-thrown into a pile of sharp rocks. He put on the clean, pressed pants hanging over the back of the straight chair and took out a checked shirt from his bedroll at the foot of the bed. The shirt went on with some difficulty over his tightly bandaged chest. The effort left him weak and breathing hard. Someone turned the meat over and it sizzled loudly.

Hunter ran his fingers through his matted hair before stepping from behind the curtain. What he needed in the worst way was a bath and a shave. Jay was bent over the stove, removing something from the oven.

He padded silently to the fire and stood with his back to the heat. He surveyed the one-room cabin for the first time and looked at Jay with unguarded eyes. The room bore the clear imprint of a woman's touch. He enjoyed special things about a woman. Like a clean-swept room, curtains, and a kitchen smelling of fresh-baked bread. These thoughts sent a pang through his chest, and the memories of Millie, usually locked tightly away, came spilling out. God, how he missed her.

Other than the huge wood stove, a table and chairs and Buck's bed were the only items in the room. Beneath Buck's bed were a few animal traps, folded fur skins of some kind, and an enormous pair of leather boots topped with quills and brightly colored beads. Hunter noted the blue lace-trimmed

41

curtains above Buck's bed and smiled. His eyes wandered back to Jay, still busy at the stove.

She wore a full-length blue dress trimmed with a white collar and covered with tiny red flowers. The dress accentuated her full figure and stirred up old feelings within him.

"Sure could do with a cup of coffee, ma'am." Jay was humming to herself, and his voice startled her.

"Oh! I didn't know you were awake. You were sleeping so soundly a few minutes ago." It embarrassed Hunter to be fussed over. He managed a lopsided grin.

"We Hunters take our sleeping seriously." Jay looked concerned.

"I'm not sure you should be out of bed yet."

"Another thing we Hunters are widely noted for—fast recuperative powers," he said with a weak chuckle. Jay eyed him benignly.

"I won't ask what else you Hunters are noted for," she said lightly, pouring him a steaming cup. The hot stove had tinged her cheeks a deep crimson, and a strand of loose hair fell stubbornly down one side of her face. She motioned for him to take the rocker by the fireplace. He eased his sore body down and gratefully accepted the coffee. She took a seat on the wide hearth across from him.

"Tastes so good," he said, sipping the strong brew. "What made you decide to come out here from St. Louis?" She looked up from her coffee cup and Hunter saw the pain reflected in those bottomless green pools. Reminded him of some wild animal with heart.

"Mother died last year and while Buck was back for the funeral I made up my mind to come back with him . . . to see for myself this strange country of rugged mountains and deserts he talked so much about."

"And?"

"I must admit, it grows on you rather quickly, almost like St. Louis is nothing more than a dream now. This place is real. You break a leg in this wild country, you could die. It's rugged, vast, and beautifully lonesome all at the same time. You understand?"

"Know exactly what you mean. Came to get away from

42

civilization and . . . bad memories myself. Trouble is, this country is beginning to be overrun with every type of human parasite known to exist. Not the miners and such, although their damage to the mountains will take decades to repair. Clear-cutting the timber where the soil can only erode and wash away is inexcusable. And dredging equipment ought to be outlawed for the damage it does. Some stream beds are changed forever using hydraulic mining to search for gold. When the streams and timber go, so does the wild game."

"Sounds as if you don't think too much of these miners."

"Some are bringing valuable skills I admit will be needed once the gold and silver pinches out. But as you probably know, there's the other types—the cutthroats, thieves, con men, and the like, who come only to take, never to give." Jay threw another chunk of wood on the dying fire, sending out a thousand red-tailed comets in all directions. The glow highlighted the soft masses of her flowing hair.

"And which are you, Mr. Hunter?" She looked at him squarely with those green eyes again.

"Please call me Jim. After what you have done for me, the mister seems too formal."

"And I'm Jay. Janett is for those I don't know well or don't like."

"Glád I'm someone you know . . . or like," Hunter probed.

Jay bent her head to her coffee demurely, leaving him to guess. "You haven't answered my question."

"Well, I'm not a lawyer or doctor, nor a dirt farmer either."

"Nor a cutthroat or thief," Jay added, "unless I miss my guess."

"No, but I'm no saint either. Raised and educated back east and served with General Grant during the war as one of his aide-de-camp personnel."

"Lost a few good friends in that horrible war," Jay said strongly.

"Most everyone did . . . friends or relatives," Hunter said softly, "on both sides." Jay got up to refill their cups. Hunter closed his eyes and thought again of the war and the haunting scene that day in the Wilderness. And of the dead man in the canyon. Something clicked and he sat up straight in his chair. Could they be one and the same? His mind worried with this bit of information for a few minutes. It was a long time ago. But something nagged at him and he tried to picture the man without a beard.

"What is it, Jim? You look strangely pale," Jay said, handing him the cup.

"It's nothing, thoughts just rambling a bit." She took her seat again, looking at him curiously.

"Those were not rambling thoughts, unless I miss my guess." Hunter looked flustered and he sipped his coffee to gather his thoughts.

"The man I shot, I believe I know him," he said softly.

"You do?"

"Well, I can't be sure, but I think I do. Happened a long time ago, place called the Wilderness. We were fighting Lee's troops just south of the Rapidan. Worst place I ever saw for tangled vines, swamps, dense thickets, and steep-banked ravines. We don't have anything out here a close second to this place. More like hell on earth once the fires started from the artillery shells . . . a smoky living hell."

"I've heard of the place," Jay said sympathetically. Hunter took another sip of coffee, running a hand through his hair.

"Place I'll never forget if I live to be a thousand. Grant gave me orders on the second day of battle to locate Hancock's troops and redirect them to the Plank Road, where Getty's men were in the hottest part of the fighting of the whole campaign. That's when I stumbled into them. Three Confederates. Place was so gloomy, I was on them before I knew it. Think they were as surprised as me. No more than ten paces stood between us, a grim-faced old man and two others looked to be a few years younger than me. It was the tall broad-shouldered youth with the red hair that I stared at what seemed an eternity but was no more than a minute or two."

"You think he could be the same man you killed a few days ago?" Hunter shook his head, doubt crowding his voice.

"Admit it's been a long time but . . . add a beard and a few lines around the eyes . . ."

"What about the other two?"

"Only one I need to worry about. The old man cut loose on me and I shot him in the face. I'm sure I killed him . . . first time for me. Still carry a scar where his bullet burned my ribs."

"Wondered what caused that when I bandaged you." Hunter grinned at her.

"Figured me to be some bad desperado, did you?"

"And what of the other man?" Jay asked, ignoring his question.

"Didn't pay too much attention to him, but what I did notice was he was short and stocky like." Hunter screwed up his face, trying to recall as much about the man as he could. Had he seen that man as well since then? He shook his head to clear it. He was going crazy to believe he could run into the same men again after so long and so far away from that place.

"So, since you are not a desperado, what is it you do?" she asked over the rim of her cup. He could say one thing for her, she never gave up on a subject.

"Own a ranch down on the Gunnison. Cattle and a few head of horses mostly."

"But isn't that Indian country?"

"Ute, but you wouldn't know it with all the miners in the area. Ouray, chief of the Uncompahgre Utes, and I have an understanding. Met him and Otto Mears when Ouray came east to talk peace with the President. Ouray is not your typical Indian chief. Social and political subjects comes easy to him and he managed to get concessions when other tribes would come away with a few worthless trinkets, medals, and a few thousand dollars for millions of acres of land. Came back and started a ranch himself along the Gunnison River."

"Do you still work for President Grant?"

Hunter considered how much to tell her. He did owe her his life. On the other hand, Nate Gage would have figured he had said too much already, but Nate wasn't sitting here looking into a pair of eyes that could melt granite.

"I do, from time to time. Guess you could call me point man. I arrange local security, meet with officials, and schedule social functions . . . things like that." He looked away from those dancing green eyes.

"And he is coming to Colorado?"

"Appreciate it if you wouldn't mention this to anyone," Hunter said, looking back into the flames.

"I'll try to keep a tight rein on my tongue at the next meeting of the Ladies' Auxiliary. Outside of a couple of chipmunks or an occasional deer, you are the first person I've seen this winter." Hunter chuckled, feeling the dull pain walk across his damaged body.

"No offense intended."

"Your wife back at your ranch?" Jay asked pointedly. Hunter was startled for a brief second, and Jay could see the sheltered pain in his eyes.

"No. She died before we could move west." His voice was low and tinged with sadness.

"I'm sorry," Jay said, feeling somewhat embarrassed. "I didn't mean to pry."

"Nothing anyone could have done. A heart defect, so said every doctor between Washington and New York. But Millie was a fighter despite her rather fragile condition. When I told her of the ranch I bought from Chief Ouray, she was ready to head west knowing if something happened on the way out, there wouldn't be anything anyone could do." In spite of the pain it brought Hunter, he found it easy talking with Jay about his wife. Something he had not done with anyone since her death.

"I'm sure the doctors did everything they could. There is so very little known about the heart, much less how to treat one."

"Yeah, I know," Hunter said soberly as Millie slid back to that special place.

The last pink rays of the setting sun lingered for a brief moment on the higher peaks before slipping down the other side. Buck watched as the last fingers of red released their hold on the mountains before stepping inside.

Buck stood the Henry by the door, letting the cabin's warmth and odors surround him. It pleased him greatly to come home to a dinner prepared by his daughter. He hated to think of her leaving, yet he knew the time would come. It was for the best. He was getting along in years and he didn't want the end to come with her left alone out here.

He noticed his daughter and Hunter seated before the fire

engrossed in low conversation and wondered if there could ever be anything between them. He had taken a liking to the boy, and, he noticed, so had Jay. The dress she was wearing told him that much. Hadn't worn it since she arrived. He poured himself a cup and joined them by the fire.

"Wal, son, figgered you wuz made of tough stuff. Course I allowed that concoction Jay gave you might a helped a little," Buck said with a grin. Buck was never one to let the conversation get too serious for long. Jay smiled and gave him a pat on his shaggy head, returning to her cook stove.

After supper Hunter and Buck sat before the roaring fire while Jay cleared away the dishes. Hunter was beginning to feel like living again.

"Saw one of them fellars today we had the set-tee with," Buck said quietly, putting a match to his pipe.

"Where?" Hunter asked, instantly alert. Buck worked the bowl until it glowed like one of the coals in the fireplace before he answered.

"He wuz ridin' high up, along the ridge, slow like, as if he wuz lookin' fer something."

"You sure?"

"No mistake. Recognize that silver-flecked stallion anywhere." Buck blew a thick cloud of blue smoke from his big lungs. "It wuz him all right. I wuz only three, maybe four hundred yards below him in a spruce thicket. Horse kicked loose a rock when he wuz directly over me. Might a missed him otherwise.

"Any ideas what he was looking for . . . maybe us . . . or me?" Jay rejoined them by the fire.

"Can't say offhand," Buck said dryly. "Could be."

"Maybe he was searching for the old Reynolds gold you told me about," Jay cut in. Buck chuckled, waving a huge paw in the air as if to discount the story.

"Fer the first couple years, every rock or varmint hole in this here gulch wuz either flipped over er dug up a-looking fer that gold." Buck patted his full stomach as he drew on his pipe, sighing deeply. "Yessiree, fer a while they wuz so many pikers up here it looked like 'nother strike wuz under way."

Later Hunter lay awake listening to Buck's snoring. He had

insisted on moving to the makeshift bunk Buck had thrown together beside his own. It was the least he could do. A woman needed her privacy even if it was nothing more than a thin curtain in a small cabin. The faint glow from the lamp behind the curtained area silhouetted her figure. She was preparing for bed, and he watched as she undressed, unable to turn away. Her full breasts and slim figure were clearly outlined against the thin material, and desire stirred deep within him. Hunter forced himself to face the wall, feeling a little ashamed of himself, yet wondering if Jay had left the light on deliberately. He felt nothing for anyone in so long. Now the burning within him surfaced once more. He drifted off to sleep with Jay on his mind.

CHAPTER NINE

Quirt threw another stick of wood on the fire, pulling the thin blanket tightly about him. Meekam lay propped against his saddle, nursing a cup of coffee while he read the three-day-old *Rocky Mountain News* Quirt had gotten while in Fairplay. Meekam smiled coldly after reading the front-page item about President Grant's impending arrival in Denver, and that it would be delayed for two days while the group hunted for big game. That suited Meekam just fine. If he could locate the gold tomorrow, they would have plenty of time to get to Denver and make arrangements before Grant arrived.

"Have any luck today?" Quirt asked, shivering in the cold. As usual, Meekam had said nothing to him since riding in to camp. Meekam took a long sip of the coffee. Somewhere in the night they heard the high-pitched wailing of a lone coyote.

"Seen some rough country today, most of it unfamiliar, until this afternoon." Quirt reached for the pot to reheat his half cup of cold coffee. "Believe I've located the canyon," Meekam said without showing emotion. He folded the newspaper in a precise manner so only the story about Grant's trip was exposed. "Trouble is, one black night ten years ago makes looking for a one-eyed steer in a stampede a lot easier than finding that gold." Quirt looked worried. What if they failed? And look where Toby was—a shallow, rocky grave in the coldest place on earth.

"Maybe I could help, now that you've located the canyon?"

"Maybe," Meekam grunted, studying the paper again. "We break camp tomorrow, regardless. Be that much closer to Fairplay. We can take the stage from there to Denver once we find the gold." Quirt nodded, sucking down half his coffee in one swallow. A strange sensation came over him, and his heart raced. Denver! Was it to be only one more step closer to his own grave? In this granite-cold place and so far from Texas.

Nate Gage was in his private berth with his coat off and his sleeves rolled up, lying on a bed a foot too short for his big frame. His salt-and-pepper hair was neatly trimmed and combed straight back. The Starr .44 was still at his belt even though it was long past midnight.

He threw the butt of an unlit cigar he had been chewing on for the last several hours into a carpeted corner, oblivious to his first-class accommodations. Gage shared the Pullman Palace car with four of his subordinates, but only two were ever off duty at one time, so there was plenty of room.

Gage flung the newspaper to the floor in disgust and stared up at the oiled-walnut ceiling, listening to the silence—one of the sources of his worry.

The train was sitting on a side rail while the President and his party made an unscheduled hunting trip for the next two days. Christ! And to think he worried about making up forty minutes. The hunting party left that morning with his three security agents providing protection for the President. He remained behind after sending a wire to Hunter in Denver and receiving no reply—the other source of his worries. He had known James Hunter too long. No reply meant trouble. Question was, for Jim or the President? Or maybe both. When it came to the President, nothing was too trivial to consider if it had an impact in some way on Grant. The President was his first thought, always.

It was said only two people commanded Grant's full attention at their own time and choosing. One and foremost was Nate Gage. Grant's wife ran a distant second.

Fidgety, Gage swung his large frame from the bed and, reaching for his hat, strode over to the North Platte Railway station office. He looked menacing in his stark white shirt and slack string tie with the Starr exposed at his belt.

Pete Thompson, U.P. dispatcher, heard the station door open and looked up sleepily from his book. He came wide awake at the sight of the big man.

"Can I help you, mister?"

"Expecting a message from someone," Gage said mildly, not recognizing the dispatcher. A shift change had obviously occurred. Gage continued. "James Hunter, from Denver." The dispatcher stared at the big man, perplexed.

"Hunter is whom I'm waiting to hear from," Gage repeated, slightly irritated.

"Ain't been no messages since I came on duty at eleven and don't expect none neither," Thompson stated in a businesslike manner. "Besides, telegraph office is just down the way, but they won't be open till seven in the morning."

Gage allowed a faint smile to play across his rock-hard features as he explained with more patience than he had shown the whole trip who he was and how important he get the message the moment it came in.

"Yessir, Mr. Gage," Thompson replied quickly. "Sorry if I acted rude, I . . ." Gage waved him off.

"Not your fault, should have introduced myself."

"Message comes in before my shift is over, I'll personally bring it over."

Gage stepped back out into the cool night air and lit a fresh cigar. In the distance he could hear the discordant sounds of a badly out-of-tune piano. He took a long pull on the cigar and watched as the blue smoke drifted lazily upward into the glittering night sky.

"Where the hell are you, Jim?"

CHAPTER TEN

The next day was cloudless and surprisingly warm, causing the snow to melt along the eaves of the cabin. Hunter had gotten up early to try to get his legs under him once again. Buck was up and gone. Other than being a little sore and stiff, he felt fit enough to sit a saddle if called to. He went out to check his horse, closing the door quietly behind him so as not to awaken Jay. Cooped up long enough, he wanted to get outside and study the lay of the land. He paused in the bright sunshine, listening to the melting snow dripping from the roof. The sound was quietly peaceful. He looked around him. The snug cabin sat among a grove of aspen and horse-size boulders on what appeared to be the widest part of the canyon floor. Slanting downward some twenty yards away, a cottonwood-lined creek, swollen from spring melt, rumbled soothingly in its flight down the canyon.

Steep rocky slopes rising some three to four thousand feet above the narrow valley supported a mixed population of aspen, ponderosa, and thick stands of lodgepole at the lower elevations. This gave way to a spruce-subalpine fir habitat higher up. The sun felt good on his damaged face, and he closed his eyes to the sights and sounds of early spring, wondering how Whip Shorely was making out. The bushes shook behind him, and he whirled around.

"Hold on, son," Buck said, "it's just me." Hunter relaxed, silently cursing himself for being out empty-handed.

"Thought you might be another grizzly come to finish me off." Buck let out a howl.

"By the looks a you, guess it wouldn't take much, fer a fact." Hunter smiled crookedly at the old trapper. Buck looked a sight. His red beard looked to be on fire in the bright sun. He explained to Hunter he had been up the canyon looking for a little color.

"Buck, just where did you see our friend yesterday?" Buck pointed upslope west of the cabin.

"See that tall lightning-struck snag a-standing above the rest of them conifers three quarters of the way up?" Hunter studied the slope carefully for a full minute before he spied the twisted gray snag of a tree a good twenty feet taller than the others.

"Got it," Hunter said, his eyes watering from the strain.

"Wal, if you foller yore line of vision straight down from there about four, oh, maybe five hundred yards, right where them pines and spruce start mixin' with them aspen. Been a-baitin' a turkey in there with corn. They's feathers and droppings all over."

"Be careful you don't bait up the two-legged kind," Hunter warned.

"Don't go a-worryin' about my topknot. This child been up against a sight worse than the likes a them two."

It was mid-morning when Buck picked up his old Henry and started out of the cabin.

"Keep the water hot, child, I won't be long. Figger that turkey is as good as in the pot," Buck said, winking at Hunter.

"I've heard *that* before," Jay shot back good-naturedly. Hunter followed Buck from the cabin.

"Keep your eyes peeled, Buck. That tall one, Joe, is dangerous and snake-eyed mean, unless I miss my guess." What he meant to say was he didn't want Buck getting hurt over something that was his responsibility.

Hunter watched as Buck crossed the creek and disappeared into a screen of green foliage. He heard Jay humming a vaguely familiar song while she cleaned up the cabin. His thoughts of her still lingered from the night. He did notice she had changed back to her normal garb of woolen pants and flannel shirt this morning. From time to time he had caught her fleeting glances. He shook his head as if to clear it of Jay, knowing it would not work. He turned his attention to the ghostly snag, Jay riding his thoughts lightly.

*   *   *

Buck moved his big frame through the spruce-fir thicket with as much ease as some wild animal. The snow, thicker here along the steep, protected slope, offered little more than a whispered protest to his moccasined feet.

The bright sunlight, heavily filtered by the dense growth, cast an eerie feeling over the place. Buck could feel the closeness, and it reminded him of his trips back to St. Louis.

The tall buildings, ever-present crowds, and houses all jammed against one another had a smothering effect on him. He disliked his stay there no matter how brief he managed to make it. To his way of thinking, that was as close to prison as he ever wanted to get.

He stopped in mid-stride; his whole body tensed, all thoughts of St. Louis washed away by the sounds of metal striking granite in the distance.

Buck stood motionless while he tried to determine the direction and distance of the sound. He considered his next move. One thing he was certain of, the noise had been man-made. A prospector most likely, he thought, yet he felt no better for having decided this. He made his way carefully toward where he thought the sound had come from, stopping just short of leaving the protection of the thicket. His eyes narrowed as he looked out into the bright sunlight. A mixture of ponderosa and Douglas fir were scattered among the broken, rocky landscape. As far as he could determine, nothing was amiss. This was the same area he had been baiting turkeys for the past week.

A movement caught his eye some hundred yards upslope in a grassy sunlit aspen grove. He studied the area intently for several minutes. Again he saw a movement or flutter. This time his practiced eye separated the big gobbler from the surrounding forest cover.

Damn! he thought. If he tried for the turkey, he would be forced to leave the protection of the thicket to get close enough for a kill. Instincts told him to stay put, but he had promised Jay a turkey supper and he was going to make good his promise. He hesitated for a long moment, and against his better judgment eased quietly from the thicket.

CHAPTER ELEVEN

Meekam and Quirt Tyler had broken camp at first light, after a hasty cup of coffee. Afterward they had ridden what seemed like hours to Quirt over jumbled rocks and through thick stands of spruce and aspen and sheer-walled canyons that blotted out the sky. To a Texan used to windswept prairies, it was impossible to determine direction in the maze of canyons and high mountain passes. Finally Meekam reined in his horse and dismounted.

"Stay here and keep a sharp lookout. There's people in that cabin down there and we don't want to spook them, leastwise not till we get what we came after."

Quirt nodded his head mutely to Meekam's instructions, looking around him. They had stopped in a fir thicket near the crest of a sharp, rocky ridge, and huge boulders lay across the rough terrain. Clumps of aspen and spruce jutted out defiantly between these large rocks, fighting for what little ground they could at this altitude. Quirt dismounted and took the reins of Meekam's horse. Meekam untied his saddlebags and slipped quietly downslope through the dense green without another word.

Quirt craned his neck trying to see past the rocks and trees for a glimpse of the cabin. Visibility was limited to a few hundred feet, and he quickly lost interest in his surroundings. He never knew he could be up so high and still feel crowded in. Glumly he found a cold rock to rest on while his thoughts turned to a warmer place.

Meekam moved steadily downslope for several hundred yards until he broke out of the dense growth and into a sparsely shaded grove of ponderosa lightly mixed with an understory of second-growth grand fir. This was the area he had seen the day before in the fast-fading light. In the cool light of day he tried to reposition himself in relation to the cabin window he had seen for only a few precious moments ten years before. Meekam surveyed the tall dead snag. Slightly tilted off its axis, a few of the tree's large roots were exposed by the digging of a marmot or badger. Keeping the cabin in sight, he eased slowly through the trees, staying parallel to the steep-sided slope.

After a few hundred yards Meekam dropped lower on the slope and worked his way back. None of the trees came close to the size he was searching for. Suddenly it hit him, and he stopped dead in his tracks. He had been looking for a *live* tree! He hurried back to the dead ponderosa with renewed interest.

The huge ponderosa leaned farther downslope than he remembered, and the once-red bark was now ash-gray and sloughing off in great slabs. He couldn't see the cabin below when he aligned himself with the dead tree, but that was probably due to the additional tilting.

Swiftly Meekam dropped to all fours and began digging among the loose rock. He would know in a minute if this was the tree or not. He resorted to using his hunting rifle to loosen several of the half-buried rocks. The metallic scraping from his efforts brought a sharp protest from a nearby steller's jay. Despite the cool weather, Meekam was sweating from the effort and excitement of maybe having one more step of his plans finalized. Moving a flat rock the size of a gold pan, Meekam caught sight of a moldy leather strap and a buckle dulled to the color of a rusting water bucket. His heart pounded hard against his ribs as he tugged on the strap while sinking the knife deeper between the rocks. The rotting strap broke under the strain and he cursed savagely under his breath. Finally he freed one of the flaps on the saddlebag, and with feverish hands he lifted it back to expose the dull yellow bars to the bright sunshine.

Buck moved like a wild animal stalking its prey, his senses acutely tuned to the sounds around him. He heard nothing further of the metallic noise, and for now it was pushed aside as he concentrated on the big gobbler. He moved only when the bird had his head to the ground, feeding. Buck edged closer, yet was still too far away for a clean kill. The gobbler worked his way behind a large rotting log, searching for insects in the bark's crevices. Buck moved closer now that the log offered a shield for his movements.

Buck brought the old Henry to his shoulder when he was seventy-five yards out. He waited patiently for the gobbler to raise his head twice before he marked the spot.

The third time, the Henry roared to life. Buck acknowledged the familiar recoil as an old friend would a clap on the back. He couldn't see through the screen of smoke the instantaneous explosion of bright crimson against the blue sky—he didn't need to. That turkey was his. Automatically he reloaded the large-bore gun without thinking.

Despite his seventy-odd years, the hunt still caused his blood to race. Buck started up the slope with a lively step, eager to see just how big a kill he had made. He patted the old Henry cradled lovingly in his arm as he peered over the log at the big feathered corpse. Buck grunted his satisfaction at the sight of the bloody stump of neck.

"Nice shot, old man," Meekam said lazily, his .44/70 aimed at the mountain man's midsection. Buck froze in place; the surprise never registered on his bearded face.

Meekam leaned against a big pine just inside the circle of shaded woods. Buck noted the heavy saddlebags.

After he had transferred the gold to his saddlebags, Meekam had started back to the horses when he was brought up short by the loud boom of Buck's gun, no more than fifty yards away.

"What you doing here?" Buck asked gruffly.

Meekam feigned surprise. "Why, you're no friendlier than the first time we met." Buck's mind was racing ahead. From his position he knew he could never bring the Henry around for a shot. He considered throwing himself behind the big log but he knew he would never make it. Snake-bit mean, Meekam's eyes never blinked and he was less than twenty steps away. Buck never doubted Meekam intended to kill him. He started to shift his foot from the log in an easy manner.

"Stand just like you are!" Meekam commanded. "Ease that cannon to the ground." Buck, with no other clear choice, complied. He crossed his arms on his propped knee, and one hand, half hidden, was enticingly close to the large knife at his belt.

Satisfied he had pulled the trapper's teeth, Meekam relaxed somewhat and pulled the shifting load higher on his shoulder.

"You live in that shack down yonder, old man?"

"What you got in them bags so heavy?" Buck asked, deliberately ignoring Meekam's question. Meekam's eyes flashed fire and his cheeks flooded a deep red.

"Goddammit! I'm doing the asking and expecting answers." A hothead, easy to rile, Buck thought. Could be he could work him up some, a calculated risk, but Buck needed some kind of edge if he was going to come out of this at all. He risked a long shot.

"You part a the old Reynolds gang, ain't you? Appears you found the gold. And I figgered it fer nothing more than a yarn."

Meekam was stung by the surprisingly accurate words, and before he could recover, he saw the old man had read him like a book.

"That's right, old man." Meekam sneered, his face dark with contorted fury. Buck read the sign in Meekam's eyes as clearly as rabbit tracks across fresh snow. The time had come to play out his hand. He had read the sign of many such men in his life. His senses were acutely aware of the many sounds around him. The high-pitched scolding of a chipmunk directed at them for invading his territory was heard over the soft sighing of a gentle breeze through the pines. The world was still vibrantly alive, and he realized he was not yet ready to die.

For an old man, his movements were still lightning quick as he shoved himself backward with his propped leg at the same time sending the big knife flashing through the bright sunlight. Buck saw the blue smoke from Meekam's rifle an instant before something smashed him in the chest. The world spun around him. He caught brief snatches of sky, tall trees, grass, and rocks long before he realized the impact of the heavy slug had knocked him backward down the steep slope. He rolled and tumbled for what seemed like an eternity before coming to rest on his back among a field of rocks not far from where he had stood in the thicket. Buck lay facing the high ridge above him, the silver-trunked aspens contrasted sharply with the inter-mingling dark-green spruces.

Searing pain spread slowly across his chest, and he heard the gurgling sounds when he took a deep breath. Lung shot. He wasn't going to make it. He would drown in the blood now filling his lungs. Calmly accepting his fate, the old trapper wondered if Meekam would bother to finish the job or just let him bleed to death. He coughed hard, the metallic taste of blood rising in his mouth. He watched as a puffy cloud floated across the high ridge, momentarily blotting out the sun.

Jay popped into his mind so vividly, Buck almost called to her. He saw the flashing smile and the way she tossed her black hair when exasperated at him. She was tough and strong like him, yet he was glad Hunter was there to help ease her pain. Buck smiled crookedly up at the darkening sky. He hurt all over now. His smile faded through the intense pain. Buck knew the looks Jay threw at Hunter. The same her mother had given him, only then he was too dumb to know the meaning. Hunter was in for a surprise.

Badly shaken, Meekam wiped the trickle of blood from the side of his cheek on the sleeve of his shirt. The razor-sharp knife had barely nicked him as it streaked past his head. The old coot was damn fast. Any slower, and it would have been him lying on the ground, bleeding on everything.

Ashen-faced, Meekam looked downslope at the prostrate figure. He saw the huge red stain on the old man's chest and the glistening white stump of bone protruding through one pant leg. He grunted his satisfaction, knowing if the old man wasn't dead yet, he wouldn't be walking out of these mountains before he bled to death, not on one leg. That ought to even the score for Toby, Meekam thought grimly as he headed toward the horses.

CHAPTER TWELVE

After Buck left, Hunter wandered down to the swollen creek among the cool cottonwoods, trying to overcome the restlessness building within him. Never one for idle activity, he needed the feel of a good horse and saddle beneath him and the smell of campfire coffee after a long day of working cattle on the Gunnison. The simple pleasures were sometimes the hardest to come by. Pleasures like that would have to wait for a spell, Hunter figured. Denver was waiting and he had a job to do.

His body might still need some mending time, but he was bursting with nervous energy and the urgency to complete his mission.

He eased himself down on a small boulder near the rushing creek, letting its sounds wash over him. It was a nice, peaceful place, but his mind kept returning to more serious matters. There were only four days left before he was to meet Nate Gage and the President in Denver. He still had to make arrangements for security, meetings with civic and political dignitaries and whatever else the President would want to do on the spur of the moment. Hunter was torn between the need to leave and the desire to stay. He was fit enough to ride into Fairplay and take the stage. So why wasn't he making plans to do so? Jay's figure from last night invaded his thoughts, and he felt the hot rush of passion rise within him and he knew the answer . . . but still, he had to go.

He looked to the big snag, wishing he had gone with Buck. Would have done him good to stretch his legs.

Jay peeked out from a curtained window at Hunter seated by the stream. She had changed into the long-sleeved dress trimmed with tiny sweetheart roses on a background of blue.

Absently she brushed her hair as she studied Hunter closely. Having cleaned up and shaved, he looked nothing like the bloodied form brought in that night. One thing that stood out even then were his sensitive pewter eyes, soft yet with a certain amount of steeliness in their depths. She watched as he tried to skip a stone across the foaming waters only to have it sink on impact, smiling warmly at this simple boyish act. It had been a long time since she had shown any interest in anyone. His rugged, clean features still carried the red scar across his jawline along with several deep bruises. She liked the way his thick, dark mustache drooped over his upper lip, adding just the right touch of seriousness to his tan features and the way he carried his lariat-lean body like coiled steel. There wasn't a thing she would change about him. Bad sign, she thought.

She dropped the curtain back into place and checked herself in the mirror once again. Her cheeks were flushed with excitement. This is silly, she thought, acting like some schoolgirl on a first date. In a day or so he would ride out, and that would be that. Jay finally admitted to herself the feelings she had for him were not merely infatuation. God knows, there had been plenty of that during her hospital days. To acknowledge the depth of her true feelings startled and annoyed her. How could she have fallen for someone so quickly? She blushed deeply as she thought of her shameless actions of last night. He had to go, this she knew. But she wanted him to know he could come back if he so desired.

She poured two mugs of coffee and, taking a deep breath, headed down to the creek. It was now or never.

Hunter did not hear her approach above the wild waters, and she saw his eyes were closed with his head thrown back to absorb the heat from the sun. For a fleeting moment she had the urge to bend down and kiss his bruised lips.

Suddenly Hunter opened his eyes, and for a second she thought she might drop the hot mugs at being caught looking with open abandonment.

"I didn't mean to startle you," she said, gathering her wits about her. "Thought you might like some coffee." He smiled at her with even white teeth as he accepted the coffee.

"Glad for the company, really." She blushed slightly,

averting her eyes from his frank stare. A loud boom echoed across the narrow valley, and they both looked up the steep rocky slope.

"Guess that answers what we are having for supper tonight," Hunter said with a grin. Buck got his turkey. He stood up to get a better look. "He's close to that snag." Hunter pointed upward for Jay. He caught the scent of her perfume, and it reminded him of the wildflowers that bloomed in early spring on the high mountain meadows above his ranch.

"Buck rarely misses," Jay stated simply. They were standing close, and Hunter looked away to keep his thoughts from flying apart.

"What's he like?"

"Who?" he asked, dumbfounded.

"President Grant." She turned her green eyes on him once more, and he could feel his senses slipping into their depths. He tried concentrating on what she had asked.

"He's short, smokes evil-smelling cigars, and has a beard." They both laughed. A warm, open laugh, something he had not done with anyone in a long, long time.

"No, silly, what's he *really* like?" Hunter's face sobered.

"Without a doubt the finest man I know. He's quiet and unassuming and cares deeply for those who work for him. During the war when Phil Sheridan and Sherman were doing their level best to bring an end to the bloody fighting, General Grant could not heap enough praise on them for their efforts. No one suffered more than Grant over the useless loss of life on both sides." He looked at her for understanding.

"I know what you mean," she said softly. "We tended to our share of wounded, both Union and Confederate. Nothing but young boys fighting for a cause few even understood."

"A lot of senseless dying occurred, there's no doubt." His thoughts flashed back to the Wilderness, to the dead man in the canyon, and finally to a lone rider on a gray-flecked horse. Hunter drained his cup, looking up at the snag with a vague uneasiness, yet not knowing why.

"What's wrong?" Jay questioned. He looked from the dead tree to her face, clouded with concern.

"It's nothing, I guess. Been cooped up too long . . . like

Buck gets sometimes," he said with a grin.

"Tell me about your ranch, who looks after it while you are away?" Hunter brightened.

"Whip Shorely. An old prospector-turned-horse-rancher who, wish I could say was cured of gold fever but doubt it. You would like him. Got more stories than a jackrabbit has relatives. The ranch is situated near Sun Creek, where it empties into the Gunnison River. Has high mountain meadows for late summer grazing and plenty of good bottomland for winter forage."

"Sounds beautiful."

"It is, but not as beautiful as you," he said soberly. The words spilled out of him naturally, without thinking. Jay blushed deeply. He felt like taking her in his arms, but he knew he had no right. The moment passed.

"So you will be leaving soon for Denver . . . the President?"

"Yes. I . . . it's my job," he said lamely.

"What you do is very important. President Grant needs you. If it weren't for him, I might've missed knowing you." Their eyes met and locked.

"Jay, I—"

The flat bark of a .44 reverberated across the narrow canyon walls, tearing their moment apart with harsh reality.

CHAPTER THIRTEEN

Hunter looked immediately to the ash-gray snag, concern clouding his features. Jay stood frozen; her eyes questioning.

"Probably some prospector looking out for his evening meal." His voice sounded flat and hollow. Not at all convincing.

"We haven't seen anyone in this canyon since winter's first snow," Jay declared, "although I suppose with the early spring melt and all . . ." Her voice trailed off to a whisper.

Hunter knew. It was too late. He cursed himself for having placed Buck in further danger.

"What is it, Jim? What's wrong?" Her words galvanized Hunter into action.

"No time to explain," he said roughly, shoving her toward the cabin. "Throw a bridle on my horse while I get my rifle. Buck may need help."

When he came out of the cabin holding his loaded rifle, he found Jay astraddle her own horse, a determined look on her face, the beautiful dress bunched up around her legs. He never questioned her right to go.

Oblivious to the pain, he pulled himself into the saddle and started across the creek as fast as he could manage. They pushed the horses for all they were worth, with Hunter cursing the jumbled rocks, wind-thrown trees, and steep bed of loose talus that slowed their progress to a crawl at times.

Hunter urged as much speed from his horse as he could stand to take, his body aching from the jolting ride.

He started in the general direction of the snag, but with all the maneuvering around deadfalls and through thick canopied forests, he was unsure of the direction anymore. They had to be getting close. But how close? And in what direction? He reined his horse in abruptly and turned to Jay as she checked her horse to keep from running him down. Even in his urgency Hunter couldn't help noticing her windblown hair and flushed cheeks. She was beautiful. He wished there were time to tell her.

"Looking for the big lightning-killed snag near where Buck's been baiting turkeys. You know the direction from here?"

She pointed upslope and slightly to his left. "About three or four hundred yards that direction." They started forward again but more cautiously. He didn't want to endanger Jay's life as well.

In a few minutes the pine-lodgepole mix thinned out and changed over to spruce. He spotted the huge gray corpse against the sea of dark green. According to what Buck had told him, the spot he was talking of should be to his left and slightly below the dead tree. Hunter jacked a shell into the chamber of the carbine as he brought his horse to a full stop. He looked back at Jay and silently their eyes met for a brief moment. He motioned for her to dismount.

Leaving their horses, he led the way on foot. They found Buck among the rocks staring upward into the blue sky. Jay stifled a cry of pain as she rushed by Hunter. He brought the hammer back to full cock, looking sharply at the surrounding trees and rocks for signs of danger. Nothing moved. He knelt down by the big trapper yet kept his ears open for first sign of trouble.

Buck was barely breathing, and thick rivulets of blood seeped slowly from the corners of his mouth, staining the rocks below.

He was in shock and Jay knew it. Her actions seemed frenzied to Hunter, yet no motion was wasted on her part as she checked his vital signs, the gunshot wound, and the broken leg. Miraculously no major arteries seemed to be severed. At least none she could see for now. She tended to his chest wound, noting that an inch lower and the bullet would have found his heart. Her mind detached itself from personal feelings, and she worked coolly over the prostrate trapper as if he were nothing more than another injured patient. Hunter felt helpless and bitter knowing the slug Buck had taken was really meant for him.

Jay ripped part of her white petticoat away. This she tore into strips and plugged the small hole in his chest.

"Help me ease him over," she commanded. Hunter sprang into action.

The exit hole in Buck's back was large and ragged. He heard the small cry of anguish escape from Jay as she bent to put the compress in place. There was a large pool of dark blood beneath the hole.

"We must get him back to the house so I can tend to his wounds properly," she said in a frightened voice, "or he is going to die." Her eyes filled with tears, and Hunter wanted to gather her to him and make the world right again, but he knew that time was past. As soon as the realization sank in that the bullet Buck had taken was meant for him, especially if Buck died, he could forget any notions he might have where the two of them was concerned.

"I'll get the horses," he mumbled.

Somehow they managed to get Buck back down the steep mountain without any of them taking a spill. The going was slow and agonizing for Buck, and it took both of them to hold the big man in the saddle. Hunter lost all track of time.

It was all they could do to get Buck in the cabin and into bed. Jay had taken most of the load. Hunter collapsed in a nearby chair, weak and spent from the exertion. Although he hurt all over, he didn't feel as though he had reopened any of his wounds.

Meanwhile, Jay worked busily over her father, cutting away the rest of his leather shirt. She cleaned and rebandaged the chest wound, her mind busy with its sinister implications. He had lost a considerable amount of blood, and she was afraid one of his lungs was badly injured and possibly collapsed.

Buck, in a state of shock and semiconscious, mumbled something as he tossed around on the bed as if trying to free himself from an unseen adversary. His usual leathery brown skin stood in stark contrast to his flaming beard. When he coughed, the deep rattle in his injured lung sounded ominous.

Hunter watched Jay work while he tried to piece together what might have happened. The rider on the gray-flecked horse flooded his mind. He knew what he must do.

"I need your help." Her voice was businesslike again. Hunter jumped to her side.

"Hold his head up, I need to get this into him. It will help ease the pain and make him sleep." She held a large amber bottle in her hand.

Jay forced the liquid between Buck's teeth. He coughed and sputtered as the thick liquid burned its way down his throat. It brought him to full consciousness.

He looked up with dull, pain-ridden eyes at Hunter. "Seems we done traded places," he whispered, a faint smile touching his lips. "Damn good thing we have a nurse in the family," he said, showing a little of his old spirit.

"Hush," Jay said, "you need to rest."

"Who shot you, Buck?" Hunter asked quickly. Buck coughed, bringing up bright blood with his saliva.

"The fellar ridin' that gray horse." Hunter swore silently to himself. Buck continued. "Seems he wuz carryin' something almighty heavy in them saddlebags . . . gold, I figger." Hunter and Jay exchanged glances.

Buck mumbled something about a gobbler and getting caught by the short hairs, and then his voice trailed off into nothingness. Hunter eased the shaggy head back onto the pillow.

"I don't know if he will make it or not," Jay replied, worried, when Hunter looked questioningly at her. Her pain was clear to see. "I've got to set his leg and get the wound stitched up while he's asleep." She had already cleaned the protruding bone and tied off a few minor vessels. The ragged leg bone was starkly white and glistened like the butt end of a wind-thrown aspen.

"I'll get some boards from the barn to set his leg." Afterward Hunter gathered up his belongings and was tying his bedroll behind his saddle when Jay stepped from the cabin. The creek was still rumbling down the canyon, where it seemed just moments before they had stood in pleasant conversation. Now all that was changed. Buck was near death, and he could see the suffering in Jay's eyes . . . because of him. Hell of a way to repay kindness, he thought bitterly.

Jay watched him silently for a moment. She could have

stopped him no more than anyone could have stopped her from going after the man who had shot her father if she were able. With the low-slung Colt buckled around him, he seemed different, more cold, and dangerous. His face was somber with a hard-edged, determined cut to it. His eyes were nearly colorless in the bright sunlight, and when he spoke, cold anger crowded his voice.

"I'm sorry for all what's happened. That don't make it right, I know." He looked from her worried face to the giant snag defying nature's last request to lie down. He slipped into his coat and turned back to Jay. "That bullet was meant for me. Buck was second choice, and he took it."

Jay silenced him with a soft finger to his lips. He hesitated for a moment and slowly took her in his arms. They held each other for a long moment in silence. He let her go and stepped into the saddle.

"I'll head for Fairplay and have the doctor out here as soon as I can." Jay shook her head.

"There's no need. Doc Lowe is nothing more than a drunken quack." She reached up to squeeze his hand. "I have everything I need here. Please be careful, James. I know how you feel, but your first responsibility is to the President. Buck would want it that way." Maybe so, but they deserved better and he aimed to see they got it.

"I'll be back" was all he could manage. He swung the buckskin around and headed back to the spot where they found Buck. Once across the creek and safely in the trees, he reined up and had a last look at the little cabin. He turned back to the steep mountain slope, his mind as cold and ruthless as a cougar stalking a mule deer. He was determined to dog their trail no matter where it took him. Buck deserved that much . . . and so did Jay.

Best he could figure, they had a solid four hours head start and as yet he didn't know their direction. He pushed the tired horse up the slope once again.

Once at the spot, he could tell Buck had fallen from above by the way small rocks had been turned over, exposing their darker undersides. He followed their path upslope some thirty yards.

Hunter found the old Henry lying on the ground by the fallen log. On the opposite side he found the beheaded turkey. Carefully he searched the area outward for a radius of twenty yards. He found the boot tracks of one other man. The boots left deep impressions in the still-spongy, wet earth. Farther out he found Buck's knife. He wasn't sure, but he thought there were tiny flecks of dried blood on the blade. He hoped so. He thrust the large knife in his belt and continued to work outward painstakingly. Part of him wanted to rush ahead blindly while the other forced him to proceed with caution and to overlook nothing important.

Hunter picked up the trail of the booted man and followed it some four hundred yards upslope into a grove of spruce and fir. There, the first man was joined by another with two horses. One a silver-flecked stallion, no doubt.

From the looks of it, they were headed over the high steep ridge. Hunter descended the rocky incline to where he had left his horse. Mounting up, he picked up the trail of the two men, moving as fast as caution would allow.

Picking his way through rocks, Hunter lost the trail a few times but always managed to find it again. It still pointed steadily upward. Soon the grand fir and aspen were left behind until nothing grew among the cold rocks but a few stunted alpine fir. Hunter buttoned his coat against the high-altitude cold, leaving the butt of his Colt free and within easy reach.

It was late afternoon when Hunter topped the high ridge. To the west the last warming rays of the setting sun fanned out slowly behind the majestic peaks of the snow-covered Mosquito Range. The clear sky was streaked with red and gold. To the east he could see the road winding its way up Red Hill Pass. He stepped from the saddle and loosened the cinch on his laboring horse. Although bred for the high country, the ride to the top had been punishing for the buckskin and as steep a vertical climb as he ever attempted. His wounds had long since settled into a dull ache; otherwise, he figured himself to be in pretty good shape.

He surveyed the valley below, looking for movement, yet keenly aware of the beauty around him. The backbone of the Mosquito Range rose sharply to over fourteen thousand feet.

Their lofty peaks, still covered with deep snow, gave way to dark green spruce, fir, and finally to naked aspen as they moved down the sides of the mountains. Still, it was not as breathtaking as his ranch. It was not unusual to see elk grazing alongside his cattle in the high meadows. The same meadows they had been grazing before the arrival of even the Ute.

A few lights were already on in Fairplay, some two but rocky miles distant. The Middle Fork of the South Platte moved sluggishly past the tiny gold camp like a huge silver snake. It would be dark within the hour and Hunter pondered his next move. There was less snow on this side of the sun-exposed ridge and their trail would be faint at best over the rocky ground. The question was, did they head to Fairplay or did they skirt the town and continue west . . . or east?

He retightened the cinch and stepped into the saddle. Guess he would never know standing around up here in the cold. He pointed the tired buckskin down off the ridge toward the inviting lights. He had gone no farther than a dozen yards when a white-tailed ptarmigan, still dressed in its winter coat, burst from the rocks near him. His normally docile horse bolted sideways and Hunter felt a tearing pain in his side. It was all he could do to keep from being thrown into the rocks. Once he had the buckskin settled down, he continued his descent, the sharp pain in his side setting his nerves on edge.

CHAPTER FOURTEEN

Hunter walked his tired horse through the fast-fading light down the main street of Fairplay. The red glow of the setting sun had long since released its hold on the Mosquito Range, and a deep mantle of purple settled down over the mountains and the valley below.

Slender shafts of yellow light raced out into the street to timidly touch Hunter as he slowly eased his horse through the gathering dusk toward a two-story hotel. The late evening chill was shattered by an out-of-tune piano, and shrieks of laughter could be heard from a large gambling establishment on his right. Heavy-booted men in miners' garb stomped up and down the street, intent on enjoying the fruits their hard work had provided.

Although Fairplay still retained the atmosphere of a boom town, it was already a dozen years old and still growing. The gold camp was so named by a group of miners expelled from other camps after all the best claims had been taken. Actually the location was not so new, since Chief Tierra Blanca of the Utes had camped regularly on the Sacramento Flats through the 1840s. After the gold pinched out at Buckskin Joe, Fairplay became the seat of Park County in 1866. And during its birth, the Confederate renegade, Jim Reynolds, established himself as camp boss for a short while. Hunter wondered if the two he was trailing were part of the old Reynolds gang. Did they really find the buried gold as Buck indicated?

Hunter knew the history of Fairplay; he had trailed a few head of cattle up from his ranch to sell to the meat-starved miners the previous fall. And for a fair price, unlike others who came with goods to sell at five to ten times the going price in Denver. For this reason he had met a few honest men, like the big rock-hard Swede, Carl Jensen, who with his brother Bo worked one of the best-paying claims in the South Park area.

These two amicable blond giants had befriended Hunter, taking it upon themselves to act as the miners' representatives, buying and distributing the meat to the nine hundred–odd miners working the gulches and streams around Fairplay. And for those miners showing little color, the Jensen brothers carried them for their share of the meat.

To thank the Jensens for their generosity and Hunter for his fair pricing, the miners threw a party for them the night before Hunter was due to leave Fairplay. The rough and tumble, hard-drinking and hard-fighting miners, their bellies full of fresh meat, put their hearts and souls into making the party a success. The miners were still going strong when the first pink fingers of early light crept silently over Red Hill Pass and Hunter headed southwest nursing a boulder-size headache.

And now, as Hunter tied the buckskin to the railing in front of the hotel, he wondered if the Jensen brothers had ever been reimbursed by the poor-luck miners. He climbed the three steps leading to the hotel and pushed his way inside. The rush of warm air, supplied by a large potbelly stove around which two old, gray-whiskered men sat talking in low tones, stung his cold cheeks and sent new blood rushing to the chilled parts. He closed the door behind him. He was stiff and sore from the unaccustomed hard ride.

Sam Colfax, hotel proprietor, glanced up from the *Fairplay Flume* and stared mildly at the man in the doorway. Recognition shot through his watery eyes.

"Well, Jee*zus!* Welcome back to Fairplay, James." Colfax threw aside the newspaper and motioned Hunter to the stove.

"How you doing, Sam?" The two shook hands. "You haven't changed a bit." The moon-faced proprietor smiled broadly. Prematurely bald, Colfax looked a good ten years beyond his thirty-five. A man unaccustomed to physical labors, his body had filled out over the years so much he looked square. His small stature tended to compound his stockiness. One thing Hunter had learned about the hotel owner—the little man had a heart of gold.

The two older men by the fire stopped their conversation to

listen to the exchange between the stranger and Sam Colfax, more out of curiosity for outside news than out of rudeness.

Hunter dropped into a chair by the stove and stretched his legs to the heat. He accepted the steaming mug of coffee from Colfax. The old men stared openly at Hunter's damaged face.

"Here," Colfax said, pouring a little brandy into Hunter's cup from a silver flask. "It'll chase away the chills a lot quicker. What brings you to Fairplay so soon in the season? More beef to sell?" Hunter shook his head as he took a long swallow of the fiery mixture. The explosion in his empty belly was a welcome relief. It perked him up a little.

Colfax studied his friend closely. "You been sick, James? You look worse than John Brown's ghost. What happened to your face?" The livid scar running the length of Hunter's jawbone was reddened by the raw cold.

"Sam, you will make someone a fine wife someday with your questions and all. Haven't you been out here long enough to know better than to ask a man personal questions?"

Colfax eased his stocky frame into a cowhide chair beside Hunter and grinned. "Only way a man knows is by asking. What's up?"

"Looking for two men," Hunter began, low-voiced. "They shot a friend of mine and left him for dead. Fact is, he may be dead by now." Silently he prayed for Buck to hang on.

Colfax took a short pull from the silver flask. "Your friend got a name?" His eyes watered from the strong brandy.

The potent coffee-brandy mixture and warm fire brought Hunter's pain and aches into sharp focus. He was a long shot from being well, he admitted.

"An old trapper, Buck Sawtelle." Colfax nodded his head. "Know him. Comes in once or twice a year for supplies. Stops by for a drink or two. Never says much, but then, I never did meet any of his breed that wasted words. Hear tell he has some kind of female type with him up there?"

"His daughter," Hunter snapped back, irritated at the implication.

"I'm afraid Doc Lowe won't be of much help. Man's got a bad liver . . . yellow as a dandelion."

"Know that. His daughter is a nurse, trained back east."

Colfax wondered how Hunter fit into all this. He never put these thoughts to words; after all, there really were times when certain questions should never be asked.

"Tell me about these gents. What brand of cayuses were they forking?" Colfax listened intently as Hunter filled him in on the details beginning with the grizzly attack and ending with Buck's shooting.

"They sound like a couple of jaspers with reason plenty to be tracking you instead of the other way around," Colfax said after Hunter mentioned the dead man, Toby.

Hunter shook his head. "Had they wanted to do that, they could have picked us off as we came out of the cabin." He didn't tell Colfax about the saddlebags.

Colfax motioned for one of the old men to come over. "At least you got a reason to look bad. Grizzly must a put up a decent fight by the looks of you."

"Monty, this here is my good friend, James Hunter." Hunter shook hands with the wiry old man. His handshake was firm and he looked at Hunter squarely with eyes the color of cobalt. Hunter liked the old man immediately.

"Monty knows all the goings-on in this town." Colfax told him of the men Hunter was after and gave him a description of their horses. "Check around town. See if anyone like them been through here the last three or four hours." Monty pulled on his fleece-lined coat. "Also, tell the Jensen boys Hunter's in town and to get over here. And while you are about it, drop Jim's horse at the livery."

Monty hurried out into the cold, glad to be doing something with a purpose again. Whoever this gent was, he didn't look the type to tangle with, Monty thought. He had seen his share of pikers come and go in these mountains over his sixty-odd years and this one, for all his softness, was granite hard underneath.

"Monty helps me out here, cleaning up, hauling wood, and the like. I give him a place to sleep and a few bucks to keep him happy. Comes in handy when you need information." He patted his ample stomach. "Might as well get something to eat over to the diner, or have you been there already?" Hunter shook his head, draining his coffee cup. He felt dragged out and too tired to move.

"Figured you heard clear down to the Gunnison about the dark chestnut beauty running the diner. Food's good and so is her looks."

They were finishing up when the two Swede brothers stomped into the diner. To Hunter they looked like two blond polar bears with smiling faces. Both were dressed in dove-gray suits that looked expensive and probably were, Hunter thought.

Carl Jensen extended his hand to Hunter. "Jim, it is good to see you again." His English was surprisingly good for someone who had been in America for only two years.

Bo spoke up. "You have brought more beef, ya?"

"Not this time," Hunter said, exchanging firm handshakes with the rock-hard men. "I'm tailing two men who shot a friend of mine. Sit down and I'll fill you in."

Colfax asked with a mouthful of food, "You boys eaten yet?" The brothers looked at each other and grinned widely.

"Ya, over an hour ago," Bo Jensen said. "Miss Buckley is the best cook in these parts."

"Yes, and the best-looking too," Carl added. "Tell us, Jim, what is this all about? Can we help?" Hunter told them of the shooting and of his trailing them down from the mountain.

"What can we do?" Carl repeated.

"I would appreciate it if you would ride out and give Jay a hand with Buck." At least if Buck died, Jay would not be alone, Hunter thought bleakly.

"You two back already?" a soft-spoken woman of about thirty asked. She was wiping her hands on a red gingham apron. The Jensen brothers looked sheepish.

"We came back for one more slice of rhubarb pie," Carl said, blushing deeply. She turned to Hunter and Colfax.

"You gentlemen care for pie as well?" Her voice was filled with an undercurrent of self-assuredness. Colfax took pie while Hunter refrained. He doubted it could be like what Jay made, regardless of the two Swedes' recommendation. He missed Jay and Buck. To him, Buck was a remnant of times long past, an anachronism, yet Hunter saw in Buck all the fine qualities this great country had been founded on—honesty, steadfastness, a strong sense of honor, and a double heaping of

75

just plain toughness. To his way of thinking, Buck still wore his bark tight.

They lingered over coffee while Hunter tried to hide his growing impatience. What next? Where did he go from here? Right now all he could do was wait for the cool-eyed Monty to bring him word.

Colfax and Hunter returned to the hotel with the Jensen brothers, who promised to look in on Jay.

Sam Colfax broke the seal on a bottle of bonded whiskey and offered Hunter a drink. He refused. There was too much to do and he wanted a clear head.

A short while later Monty hurried through the door, the expression on his wind-rawed face indicating that he was carrying news. Colfax thrust a glass of the premium whiskey into his chilled hands. Monty took it in one swallow, smacking his lips. It had been a long time since he had sampled anything this good. Hunter became impatient.

"What did you find out?"

"Plenty," Monty replied, still breathing the headiness of the news deep into his lungs. "Barstowe down to the livery recalled the two fellars right off. Showed up to his place early afternoon. Left their horses and gear, paying for a week's care. Bart showed me the horses and they's just as you described except plum wore out and wind-broke. Flatland horses, I'd swear to it. Won't be worth the pay to feed 'em."

"Go on," Colfax urged, noting the strained look on Hunter's face.

"Well, Bart said they asked when the next stage left for Denver." Hunter's features flattened out somewhat. Denver was a big place to track two men. But at least it was the direction he needed to go.

"They take the two o'clock stage?" Sam Colfax asked. Monty looked at Hunter and then at his boss, nodding his head mutely. A dejected look settled over Hunter.

"Thanks, Monty," Colfax said, pouring the old man another glass of the blended whiskey. Monty walked back to his friend by the fire as carefully as he could, holding the glass as if it were nitro. Colfax placed a pudgy hand on Hunter's shoulder. Hunter stirred.

"Sorry, old man. If you want, I know two good men to ride with you? Go myself but—" and here he patted his middle—"I would only slow you down." Hunter stood up.

"Thanks, Sam, for the offer, but this is something I have to do myself. Appreciate the help from you and the Jensen brothers. I'll need a fresh horse in three hours. You have a room I can use?"

"You got it." Colfax walked behind the counter to retrieve a key. "First door on the left at the top of the stairs. I'll wake you myself."

Sam Colfax watched as Hunter slowly climbed the stairs, his mind busy with the few pieces of the puzzle he knew.

CHAPTER FIFTEEN

A stagecoach being pushed hard through the blackness slowed down to cross Tarryall Creek before pulling into the relay station. The driver dropped to the ground as the station-master came out of the two-room cabin once owned by a prospector when placer mining was still profitable along the creek.

"How's the trip going, Clint?" the stationmaster asked as he finished buttoning up his mackinaw.

"Quiet" was Clint Loper's only comment as he opened the stage door. "Coffee's hot inside. Might as well wait where it's warm till we change teams."

The passengers dismounted from the stage, looking around them carefully. Dressed in cowhands' garb, they shook the stiffness from their limbs before entering the cabin. Clint noticed the tall one and the saddlebags he clung to tightly. That meant only one thing to Clint—gold. Either dust or bullion. He had seen the signs before. The silent, watchful eyes and guns at the ready. Trouble is, neither of them looked to be miners. The short one had the unmistakable stamp of a Texas cowpuncher. Loper was willing to stake a month's wages neither of them knew how to use a gold pan much less a pickax.

Clint Loper had driven stages now nearly twenty-four years, starting back when he had caught the fever and found himself in Sacramento in forty-nine, starving with little color to show for his labors. These two were not prospectors and he should know. He had hauled his share as stage driver between Sacramento and Mormon Island, near John Sutter's mill.

After that he helped establish relay stations with John Butterfield along the 795-mile-long Oxbow Route starting at St. Louis and Memphis and trekking past El Paso and Fort Yuma to Los Angeles and San Francisco. The stage flyer stated it cost two hundred dollars per passenger and took twenty-five days for the trip. Clint knew better. The first stage to reach California had made it in exactly twenty-four days, eighteen hours and twenty-six minutes. He ought to know. He had been the driver back in 'fifty-eight.

The stationmaster came up, leading a fresh team. "Here, let me finish. Go grab yourself a hot cup of coffee."

"Thanks, Ed. Could do with a cup. Old bones can't take the cold like they once could." As he entered the station he noted the two passengers sitting at a back table, silently watching the door. It was then Clint made up his mind about the two. They were hiding something. Either a shady past or a very recent crooked beginning. He poured himself a strong cup and stood with his back to the stove. The heat went to work on his aching joints. Had he known what the two silent men were planning, Clint Loper would not have rested so easy.

Jay sat beside Buck, listening to his labored breathing. His skin was pale and beaded with sweat. She thought back to when she first arrived in Colorado. It hadn't taken long to fall in love with the place, the people, and the mountains Buck loved so much. Looking down now at the gentle giant whose life was slowly ebbing away, she realized how happy these last few months had been. She was the tonic the old trapper needed and he the loving father she came to know and love deeply. Jay didn't want it to end. Not this way.

She did everything she knew to do for Buck, but he had lost so much blood. Blood that needed to be replaced. If only they were in St. Louis. Instantly she knew Buck would not want to be there . . . even if it meant certain death. Slowly Jay got up to throw another piece of wood on the fire and to make herself a cup of tea. The little cabin seemed so lonely even with Buck here. She missed Hunter and hoped he was safe. Silently she prayed for his return. His eyes held a lot of unspoken truths and feelings for her. The same ones she had for him as well. Whatever the future held she would accept with quiet dignity. Jay returned to Buck's side with the hot tea and placed a soft hand on his fevered brow.

CHAPTER SIXTEEN

True to his word, Samuel Colfax had his personal horse with Hunter's saddle cinched tight ready at the railing when Hunter stepped into the cold night air. The horse was a big, wide-shouldered black that looked to have plenty of bottom. Hunter tied his bedroll behind his saddle and placed the packet of food Colfax had given him in his saddlebags. The horse pranced about along the railing.

"I won't forget this, Sam." Hunter mounted the nervous animal. "I'll see you get your horse back."

Sam Colfax waved a thick hand in the air. "No need. When you get to Tarryall relay station, just before Kenosha Pass, you'll be needing a fresh mount. Tell Ed I said to lend you that big roan he keeps so fat. Do it good to run some of the tallow off. Good luck, Jim, and be careful."

Hunter reined the black away from the railing and gave him his head for the first couple of miles out of town and then settled him down to a steady ground-eating canter through the wide, flat valley as they headed for Red Hill Pass. It was bitter cold and the bright stars seemed low enough to touch. The big horse seemed to know the well-traveled toll road, and Hunter allowed him a little more lead. The road, Colfax had said, was built by a private company and extended from Fairplay to Cherry Creek and cost a dollar and seventy cents to travel.

The relay station was dark and silent when Hunter forded Tarryall Creek and rode up to the corral. He had no idea of the time. The black was breathing heavy from being pushed hard the last few miles. He stripped his gear from the horse and wiped him down with a gunnysack he found hanging on the fence. He turned the black into the corral, noting the stage team and the big roan. They eyed each other for a moment across the pale moonlight. The horse was sleek and too fat to suit him and would not hold out as the black had.

Hunter strode over to the station and banged on the door. He hated to wake a man, yet he had no choice. Something crashed to the floor behind the door and he heard a muttered oath. A yellow light appeared in the window. Hunter stepped clear of the door into the moonlight.

A balding man in dirty longjohns opened the door, holding a coal-oil lamp in front of him. He stepped out to get a better look at the man in the pale light. The stranger was tall and he wore a gun over the outside of his long coat.

"You Ed, the stationmaster?"

"Uh-huh," the scrawny man replied nervously. He shifted from one bare foot to the other on the cold planking.

"Name's Hunter. Sam Colfax said you could lend me that big roan of yours." The man stared at the stranger for a moment, his eyes sliding past him to the shadowy corral. The outline of another horse could be seen.

"Come inside before I freeze to death." Inside, Hunter removed his heavy coat. "I'll heat up the coffee." Hunter dropped into a chair near the fire. The stationmaster disappeared into the next room and came out pulling on a dingy pair of overalls over a faded checked shirt.

"Been ridin' most of the night?" he asked Hunter.

Hunter stood up, took a cup from near the stove, and poured a mug of the half-heated coffee. With the cup to his lips, Hunter looked over the rim at the older man.

"Didn't steal Sam's horse, if that's what you fretting over. Colfax said you would lend me the horse and to tell you he would send someone out in a few days for his." His patience was wearing thin.

"Reckon you're right. If you had a mind to steal him, you would a been long gone by now."

"I'm trailing two men. Shot a friend of mine up in Handcart Gulch."

"Buck Sawtelle?"

"Afraid so. His daughter's caring for him."

"That a fact? Heard old Buck had hisself a woman up there, but I didn't know why." Ed grinned. "Figgered him and me was

81

long past the point of needing a female varmint anymore." Hunter ignored the comment.

"Did you happen to notice two men on the last stage? One looks like he wouldn't turn his back to his own mother."

Ed's eyes lit up. "They came through here all right. The tall one was just like you said. Clinging to saddlebags like his life depended on it."

"Did they say anything or did you overhear any of their conversation?"

The stationmaster shook his head. "Nary a word. Sat right over there against the wall, drinking coffee and a-staring at the door like the first cavalry was fixin' to bust through any minute."

"Who was driving the stage?"

"Clint Loper, a good man."

"Where can I find him once I get to Denver?"

"Best ask at the depot. Lives somewheres out on Cherry Creek. All he ever told me."

"Thanks . . . for the coffee and the information," Hunter said, draining his cup. Ed eyed Hunter curiously, wondering if he was a lawman or simply a friend of Buck's. By the looks of him, Ed pegged him as a law dog. Hunter pulled on his coat.

"You take the roan, mister. Lord knows he needs ridin'. Buck and I go back a long ways."

"I'll see you get him back."

"Don't worry yourself none. Tell Jack Needam at the Elk Creek relay, about forty miles from here, to lend you one of his and you should make Denver in record time. Tell Jack to tie my horse to the next stage headin' this way. I'll do the same to Sam's."

The big roan surprised Hunter. The horse was willing to run, and Hunter alternated between a fast canter and a full gallop for over a dozen rough miles. The roan had a wide stride that ate away at the miles. His sore body had long ago settled into a numbness he no longer felt unless he made a sudden move.

The day broke clear and Hunter figured he was no more than a few miles from Elk Creek station. The bright sun lifted his sagging spirits somewhat. He wondered if Buck was still alive to enjoy it.

The toll road was crowded with miners and equipment-laden wagons headed west. Some were rough, experienced miners, but most were as new to the fields as the boots they wore and the pickaxes they carried. Probably bought in Denver at exorbitant prices, Hunter figured.

Hunter shook his head at the folly of some men. He knew from experience only few had what it took to survive the rough ways of a miner. Most would either be busting their backs in a company mine for low wages before first snow or headed back east, broke and disillusioned, their dreams of riches crushed like ore in a stamp mill. There never *was* enough gold to go around.

At the Elk Creek station, Jack Needam balked at lending Hunter a horse. Since his was the last station on the line, Needam figured he would never see his horse again.

"No offense, young fellar," Needam said, working a boulder-size chew to one side of his mouth to shoot a stream of dark liquid at a large harvester ant. The ant took a direct hit. "Your intentions may be good, but once you get to Denver, among all the hullabaloo, you might forget where you got him." Then he added quickly when he saw the expression on Hunter's face, "Now, I ain't saying you would," and held up a bony hand.

"How much?" Hunter asked through rising anger. He was tired, irritated, and in a hurry.

"Well, got me a couple fine hawses over to the corral I recently bought offin' a miner passin' through." Hunter had no doubt of the direction the miner had been heading. "Could let you have one fer, say, fifty dollars."

Hunter shifted his eyes to the two animals in the pen. They were rough-looking just coming out of winter. One was a paint, the other a gray. Both were old mustangs and about used up. Hunter hadn't figured different.

He turned to Needam with fire in his eyes. "Do I look that green?" he said evenly.

"I'll admit they—" Hunter cut him off.

"Twenty for the paint and another twenty dollars for some information." Needam perked up. He had given the miner only ten for both mustangs. He nodded, more worried he might not

83

have anything worth telling for the double eagle. Hunter gave him the money for the horse and began flipping the gold coin in the air. The dull gleam reflected in the bright sunlight struck the old man in the eyes. He stood rooted to the spot, mesmerized by Hunter's actions.

"Were there any passengers on today's stage for Denver? Not the one just left Fairplay, the other one." Needam stared at the flying coin.

"Two. Looked to be a couple drovers."

"Describe them." Needam's descriptions were accurate. Hunter felt his pulse quicken. At least they were still heading toward Denver. He worried they would drop off at some point and he would miss them on the trail.

"Now, think carefully. Did they say anything to you or did you overhear talk between them?"

The old man felt uncomfortable under Hunter's hard stare. His eyes made a man feel as if he had bared his soul to the world.

"The big one asked if I had a copy of the *News*. Told him I couldn't read," Needam said sheepishly, "didn't need no newspaper."

"Anything else?" Hunter probed. He had stopped flipping the coin.

"Only if I knew if the President's trip was still on schedule," Needam said offhandedly. "Guess everyone wants to be there when he arrives."

"What!" Hunter asked harshly. He seized the old man by his shirtfront with both hands. All the color drained from Needam's face as he stared into Hunter's hot-steel eyes. At close range, tiny flecks of gold seemed to be floating in the molten gray.

"Think carefully. What were your exact words to him?"

Their faces were less than a foot apart and a deep nauseating sense of fear spread upward in Needam's guts. Forget the money. All he wanted was to be free of this man with the burning eyes.

"Told him what I had heard," Needam said barely above a whisper. "Grant was off a-huntin' somewheres. Two, maybe three days behind schedule. All that was ever said after that.

Ate their meal and got back on the stage. Honest to God, mister, that's all I know." Hunter finally realized he had the old man jerked up so tight he was standing on his toes.

"Sorry." Hunter pressed the double eagle into the man's callused hand. Needam tried to refuse the money.

"No, you take it. What you've said could be worth a lot more." The old man blinked his eyes in total confusion.

Hunter left the Elk Creek station in a cloud of dust. The mustang, surprised at the spurs put to him, responded with a gut-bottomed courage that took him back to his days of chasing cows from Texas to the railhead in Wichita. Hunter urged all he could from the little paint. It was more important than ever he get to Denver now. For some reason the two were interested in the President of the United States, and that worried him greatly. If the President stopped for a hunt, it was as a favor to the group. Hunter knew Grant did not care for hunting. This change in schedule and the fact Nate had not heard from him probably had Nate in a foul mood. Such inconsistencies had a way of gnawing at Nate, but it did have one positive effect. It put him on double alert, and that was good. As if sensing Hunter's urgency, the little paint increased his speed.

What connection could the two men he was following possibly have to the President? If they were trying to lose someone after a shooting, why head straight to Denver? If what Buck said was true, they had enough gold to live like kings. Could it be their objective was the President all along, and the run-in with Buck and himself nothing more than an inconvenience growing out of the death of a man named Toby? Hunter's guts were tied in knots, and he felt a growing sense of foreboding where the President was concerned.

CHAPTER SEVENTEEN

At that moment Nate Gage was leaning back on two legs of a straight chair outside the telegraph office, smoking a thin black cheroot. He had sent a wire to the U.S. marshal in Denver, since he had not heard from Hunter. It was up to him to arrange security for the Denver portion of the trip. Nate brought the chair down hard. Tilting the flat-brimmed black hat back on his head, he squinted in the afternoon sun out across the tracks the hunting party had made. Nothing moved on the treeless landscape. He threw the half-smoked cheroot into the dusty street in disgust. North Platte. He was beginning to hate the place. He worried about Grant and the unscheduled hunting trip and the nagging conviction Hunter was in trouble.

He stood up, deciding to walk down to the saloon and have a beer while he waited for the marshal's reply. Gage adjusted the dark pinstriped coat over the handle of the Starr. He stuck his head into the telegraph office and told the dispatcher where he could be found when his message came in.

Charlie Farnsworth looked up from his desk at the big man. "Yessir," he replied quickly, even though he knew he wasn't obligated to go running all over town delivering messages. But he also knew who the imposing figure was, as did everyone in town. If Charlie had been asked, he would deliver the message to the very gates of hell.

An hour later Farnsworth hurried through the doors of Big Jake's saloon and over to Gage, who sat at a corner table with a half-empty beer glass before him. The first and only one he would drink while on duty. Farnsworth handed the wire to Gage and left not expecting a reply. Gage unfolded the wire and read:

NATHANIEL GAGE STOP ANTICIPATING HUGS
ARRIVAL STOP PRELIMINARY STEPS TO SECURE
TENDERED STOP WILL ADVISE HUNTER STOP
WAITING ARRIVAL STOP

Frank Bounds
US Marshal

Gage tore up the wire. Good man, Bounds. At least he had
begun to establish some security procedures. The reference to
"HUGS" was Gage's way of keeping a low profile in matters
dealing with President Grant. If messages were intercepted by
unauthorized persons, few would even suspect "HUGS"
referred to the President of the United States. The use of the
term was a holdover from the war, when Gage and Hunter used
it to report troop movements for Grant. The letters stood for
Grant's full name, Hiram Ulysses. Through a clerical error his
name had been changed to Ulysses Simpson Grant when at
West Point. Grant never bothered to correct the mistake, and
soon fellow cadets began calling him "Uncle Sam" later
shortened to just "Sam." Few knew him except as U. S. Grant.

Gage retraced his steps to the sidelined presidential train. As
he drew abreast of his coach, he scanned the horizon once
again. This time he saw tiny moving dots surrounded by a thin
layer of dust. It was the right direction. He climbed on top of
the train for a better view. His nerves tightened and he lit a
fresh cigar while he waited for the dots to grow.

The plume of dust grew thicker as the group of horsemen
broke into a full gallop the last mile. Gage squinted into the
slanting rays of the afternoon sun. He could see Grant in the
lead, and he relaxed somewhat. They thundered up to the train
just as Gage reached the ground. He was immediately
surrounded by a cloud of choking dust. Gage grimaced, slightly
irritated. The suit had been freshly cleaned that morning.

As the dust settled, Grant looked down from the big white
horse at his special assistant with a mixture of devilment. Like
his wife, Gage could always tell when Grant had taken just one
drink. A half-smoked cigar was clenched between Grant's
bearded jaws.

"How you been, Nathaniel?" The other riders sat their

horses waiting for the President to dismount. "You look worried, as usual."

Nate Gage allowed a grudging smile to touch the corners of his mouth. "Doing fine, Mr. President, now that you are back."

Grant stepped down from his horse and the others followed. "How was the hunt, Mr. President?" Gage asked more for the other dignitaries than for Grant. He knew where Grant stood on hunting. Grant had his hat off, halfheartedly trying to beat the tan dust from his dark clothes.

"Dry out there, Nathaniel. Everyone seemed to enjoy themselves, didn't they, Sidney?" Sidney Dillon, the stern-faced, flat-lipped Union Pacific director, had his hat off and was busy mopping the grime from his face with a silk handkerchief. At three inches over six feet, the white-haired man was more accustomed to fine offices than to traipsing over the dry countryside for game. Dillon mumbled his agreement, yet Gage could see the truth reflected in his eyes.

"Doc here was the first to bag an antelope," Grant continued, indicating a slightly stooped man of average height with a mustache and goatee. A medical doctor by training, Thomas C. Durant was also the vice president of the U.P. He smiled at being the center of President Grant's momentary attention.

"I used the President's old Sharps .45/120. The one given him by Zeb Stuart. Kicks like a mule." Even though Durant was speaking directly to him, Gage chose to ignore the little man's comments. He neither liked nor trusted the doctor.

"Suppose we get cleaned up and have ourselves a party tonight, seeing how we have an ample supply of fresh meat?" Grenville Dodge said to the President. A retired general, Dodge went back a long way with Grant, and the two were genuine friends. The President agreed.

"Walk me to my car, Nathaniel." Grant relit the obviously old cigar. The thing smelled horrible. "What's the matter?" Grant asked his aide.

"Just wish I could hear from Hunter."

"Well, I'm sure Jim has his reasons. He's a good man and can take care of himself."

"Him I don't worry about. His job is to handle advance security, and so far he hasn't done that."

"Okay, Nathaniel, I didn't mean to make light of it. You handle it like always." Gage nodded his appreciation.

"Will you see to the arrangements for tonight? Make sure you invite the mayor and anyone else you think advisable."

"You want to pull out in the morning, Mr. President?" Gage hoped so. He was beginning to hate the place.

Grant stopped in front of his Pullman, and taking a long draw on the cigar, he looked westward down the endless track.

"Let's get out of here," he said quietly. "I'm ready to see the high country. Frankly this place is kind of depressing." Grant added with a sly smile as he pulled himself aboard the train, "If you tell anyone that, I'll personally shoot you with Zeb's gun myself."

CHAPTER EIGHTEEN

Meekam and Quirt Tyler arrived in Denver a few hours ahead of the pursuing Hunter. Meekam squinted in the early morning sun that filled the interior of the coach, surprise registering on his hard features as he took in a Denver barely resembling the budding one he had last seen over ten years before. Brick buildings, horse-drawn streetcars, and gas streetlamps replaced the mud-chinked cabins and tents. He hoped he could still find his way around.

They retrieved their bedrolls from the coach's boot. Meekam slung the heavy saddlebags over his shoulder and started toward what looked to Quirt to be the seedier part of town. Actually it was that part of town where Denver had started its humble beginnings on Cherry Creek. Neither man had spoken for hours, and Quirt wondered glumly where they were heading, realizing for the very first time he no longer controlled his own destiny. He pulled the thin jacket together at the throat to keep out the early morning chill. What he wouldn't give for the hot, parched dirt of West Texas right now. His eyes were gritty from the lack of sleep and he was exhausted from the bumpy ride.

Presently Meekam turned into the open doorway of a saloon. Quirt couldn't believe his eyes, once inside. Meekam left him gawking and strode up to the longest and most ornate bar Quirt had ever seen. To his left was a large raised stage complete with long plush curtains. They were slightly parted, and he could see the highly polished floor behind them. Nothing like this back in West Texas, Tyler thought as he headed for the bar. He overheard the bartender's comments to Meekam's question.

"Mr. Chase is visiting Central City and isn't expected back

until late tomorrow." He looked nervously at the two men, wondering if trouble lay ahead. Meekam stared at the man in silent thought for a moment. Chase, a Southern sympathizer, wasn't around, so he was forced to play his ace in the hole.

"You boys want a beer?" the bartender asked as if to ease unspoken tensions. Quirt opened his mouth to speak, but Meekam cut him off.

"Madame Vestal's tent saloon still around?"

"Just down the street, you can't miss it," the bartender said, hoping to spur them on their way. The one with the cold eyes was pure poison. A double-fanged sidewinder if he ever saw one. And he had seen his share lately in Colorado.

Meekam shouldered the saddlebags once more and without further comment headed for the door. Quirt exchanged looks with the bartender and hurried after Meekam, wishing they had at least had one beer. Christ! Meekam spooked his nerves some, and a beer would have hit the spot.

They moved back onto crowded Blake Street. Quirt looked back at the classy Palace. Probably had some nice women in there. He licked dry lips, intending to find out once Meekam got whatever was in his craw out, so's they could have some fun. The street was lined with men of all descriptions, and painted ladies called out to them from their one-room cribs or parlor houses lining the street. Quirt took it all in with ever-growing desire. As far as he could tell, Meekam took no notice of the blatant advertisements.

Meekam surveyed the enormous tent saloon that had made Madame Vestal so popular for so long, and a cold smile touched his lips. Although they never formally met, he had stood guard one dark night while she spent time with Jack Reynolds. That had been in St. Louis. Later Reynolds told Meekam her real name, and after the war was over he was bringing her west to set Colorado on its ear. Too bad Jack never lived to see his dream come true; even he would have been surprised at the extent of her success. Meekam figured what he knew ought to be worth something.

Madame Vestal had indeed made a name for herself upon her arrival in the Colorado Territory. An expert twenty-one dealer, many a miner or cowboy lost money to her just to hear her heavy southern voice. It was also widely known she ran honest gaming tables and her whiskey was never cut by water or colored by plug tobacco.

Quirt entered the huge tent on the heels of Meekam. Madame Vestal's was nothing like the Palace. There was no stage or fancy curtains and the bar was nothing more than rough planking thrown together. Quirt knew where he wouldn't be spending his time. A small crowd gathered around the roulette and blackjack tables. They made their way to the bar, drawing a few curious stares.

A big, hawk-faced bartender in a fancy white shirt with black garters around his muscle-bound biceps stood wiping down the bar.

"What'll it be, gents?"

Quirt spoke first, not to be outdone again. "Couple beers." He caught the annoyed look from Meekam. Hell, he didn't care. He needed a drink to cut the dust from the long ride. And he was getting tired walking around on eggshells for Meekam. He wasn't light-headed like Toby, and it was high time Meekam realized this. The hasty gulps of cold beer bolstered his false sense of bravery.

"Is that Madame Vestal over there?" Meekam asked casually, gesturing to the brunette in the long evening gown. She laughed at something someone said. The laugh was soft with a deep, rich resonance. Meekam could see where men could be taken in by her charms. She was beautiful.

"Her all right. You aiming to mix cards with her, you better be prepared to lose," he stated matter-of-factly. "Never seen her equal when it comes to the boards."

Meekam's eyes left the woman and settled squarely on the beefy bartender. "Need to speak with her."

"Mister, you ain't the only man wishing to sweet-talk Madame Vestal, so get in line." With that he moved off down the bar. Meekam's anger blazed up momentarily at having been brushed off so easily.

He unshouldered the saddlebags and fished in his pocket for pencil and paper and scribbled a note. Folding the paper, he picked up his beer and downed it in one swallow.

"Bartender, another beer," he called loudly. The bartender

frowned but moved to oblige. Quirt gulped his down as well.

Meekam handed the note to the bartender as he put fresh beers before them. "Deliver this note to Madame Vestal," he ordered, and he laid a double eagle on the bar. "Keep the change."

"I don't know," the bartender said stupidly, looking over at the busy woman. "She don't like to be interrupted less it's real important."

"It is," Meekam said evenly. The bartender hesitated, then picked up the coin and slipped it into his pocket. Meekam watched as the note was delivered and saw a faint trace of irritation cross the woman's face when the bartender handed her the paper. A pink flush spread to her cheeks as she read it. She said something to the bartender and he gestured in Meekam's direction. She looked at him with unveiled fire in her eyes. She said something else and the man came scurrying back to the bar.

"Madame Vestal said for you to wait in her office and she would be along directly." The bartender pointed to a door at the end of the bar. Whoever this gent was, he better be ready for a tongue-lashing from the looks of his boss. And as if to distance himself from the fracas sure to follow, he moved farther down the bar to wash glasses.

"Stay here and don't do any talking." Meekam shoved the full beer to Quirt, reached down for the saddlebags at his feet, and headed for the private office. He could feel the woman's eyes boring into his back.

A short while later Madame Vestal burst through the door, slamming it behind her.

"Just who the hell do you think you are?" She screamed at him with eyes blazing. "Coming into my place with a note like this! How dare you!" She spit fire in all directions. Meekam realized how beautiful she was at close range. A large pear-shaped diamond hung in cleavage formed by the expensive red satin gown she wore.

"Don't ever use that name in reference to me again. I did what I had to do out of love for the Confederacy. Unlike you and Jack, who robbed for nothing more than to further your own personal gain."

Meekam's face flushed dark and his eyes locked on hers.

"Sit down, whore!" It was a voice meant to be obeyed. His eyes were slitted like a snake's and she sobered somewhat; the note still suspended in her hand read,

Belle, do you still miss Jack?

Meekam's hand snaked out and seized her wrist, his cold eyes boring into her. The grip was like that of an eagle holding its prey. She winced at the pain, forgetting her own righteous indignation for a moment.

"Sit!" he hissed, and let go of her arm. She stumbled backward to her chair behind the polished ornate desk, the crumpled note still clutched in her hand.

Meekam spoke in a cold, measured voice. "Belle Siddons, the infamous Confederate spy of St. Louis. Commendable job, as I understand it. Even got yourself thrown in prison by General Curtis." Meekam laughed at the stricken look on her face. "Hell, little lady, don't look so frightened. I even spent time in jail myself, although not for such an honorable act as yours."

"Somehow I never doubted that," she shot back.

Meekam held up a hand. "Before this gets out of hand, let me say I don't intend to tell anyone of your past. I simply need your help in locating a few trustworthy men." Belle snorted, her old spirits returning.

"No one would believe you if you did."

Meekam nodded. "Probably true, but there is a lot of folks out here from back east could harm your business. After all, socializing with a Southern spy kinda goes against the grain for most blue-belly soldiers."

"What about these men you need? Why not hire them yourself? Why come to me?"

"Because I figured you would know of a few good men from the South don't mind taking risks if the money is good. What I have planned could further the South's cause greatly and maybe help ease some of the pain for those lost to the war." Billy smiled at him from the grassy field.

Belle Siddons studied him for a full minute, intrigued by what the stranger was saying. Then it hit her.

"You were there that night. Now I remember you. In the shadows, sitting proudly on your horse, waiting for Jack and me to finish." Meekam nodded his head. "And everyone thinks all the old Reynolds gang are dead," she whispered.

"Except for me, they are. Meekam's the name."

Her eyes narrowed. "Where do I fit in?"

"Like I said, I need a few good men." Meekam unbuckled one side of the saddlebags and lifted out an ingot of gold. He placed it on her desk in front of her. Her eyes widened at the sight of the bar.

"You found Jack's gold as well. No wonder you can afford to pay well." Meekam shook his head.

"Hid this myself. Not even Jack knew about it. That one is yours."

Belle studied the dull bar for a moment before shaking her head. "No, I don't want or need your money, Mr. Meekam. If what you say is true, I'll see to it you get your men. But"—she paused to hold him with her ice-blue eyes—"if this is a trick, I'll have you horsewhipped and shot."

"No trick, lady. Couldn't be more serious." Meekam put the gold bar away. "I need to talk to them tonight," he added.

"What is it you are about?"

"Best you don't know."

Belle nodded her head. "On that you are probably right. Come back tonight and use the side entrance. No use arousing too much curiosity."

Meekam checked them into a cheap hotel just a few streets over from Madame Vestal's saloon. He bought a copy of the *News* and retired to his room after they had gotten something to eat.

Quirt sat glumly on the edge of the flimsy bed, the food having taken the glow from the three beers. He was tired, scratchy-eyed, and needed a shave and bath in the worst way. Yet he didn't feel like moving. He lay back across the bed, closing his eyes for a moment. Tomorrow he would get his share of the gold. And none too soon to suit him. If he was going to die, then, by Jesus, he wanted to raise some Texas-style hell first. His thoughts drifted back to home and the warm spring days he and Toby spent as children along the Calamity River.

CHAPTER NINETEEN

Saddle-weary, Hunter approached the outskirts of Denver at a slow walk, the hard-ridden mustang trembling with exhaustion. Hunter was surprised the city had grown little since his visit the year before. A couple of new buildings stood at the edge of town, but for the most part, Denver, like the rest of the country, was wallowing in a full-scale recession. A recession set off by reckless speculation and shady dealings among bankers and businessmen. For all intents and purposes, the Denver banks had suspended business. Denver suffered further from the dwindling supply of ready gold as the easily worked surface deposits of blossom rock played out. And Denver had been running at full steam on the heady metal for a long time. Business was so bad, the old Overland stage had stopped running for lack of passengers and freight.

It seemed to Hunter the only businesses not suffering were the saloons and brothels. He urged the tired horse down Larimer Street and crossed the bridge once separating the fledgling towns of Cherry Creek and Auraria. He then turned up Ferry Street and stopped at Uncle Dick Wootton's Hotel and Western Saloon halfway down the block. He had spent his time in Wootton's last year and had taken a genuine liking to the large, burly man whose rough-and-ready style reminded him of Buck Sawtelle.

Hunter dismounted stiffly and leaned against his horse for support. He couldn't remember ever being so tired. He stepped into the saloon and was greeted by Wootton's massive body, his feet propped on a table, dozing in a quiet corner. A few stragglers from the night before were playing cards. Hunter slipped into a chair beside the snoozing Wootton.

"Could sure use a shot of that lye you call whiskey," Hunter said softly.

"What . . . who?" Wootton sputtered, trying to focus his bloodshot eyes.

"Jeezus, Jim, how the hell are you?" Wootton said, shifting his big feet to the floor with a bang. His booming voice trailed off as he got a good look at Hunter's face. "What war party you tangle with?" Hunter held up his hand.

"Need a strong drink. Been riding all night." Hunter didn't care if it was only half past ten in the morning.

"Got just the ticket." Wootton fetched a large, dusty bottle from behind the bar and two glasses. "Taos lightning. Either cures you or kills you . . . and you won't care which comes first." It took two shots of the potent liquid before Hunter felt like talking. Wootton listened intently while Hunter explained what he was doing in Denver.

Wootton raised his glass. "Buck Sawtelle is one helluva trapper, and I should know. Shared a cabin one winter in Ute country. Out setting traps when a small war party pinned me down just before dark. Buck slipped up to them and all hell broke lose. Saved my topknot, he did. Yessir, they ain't a better man ever set a trap. You want my help, you don't need to ask more than once."

"I'm asking. Know Buck would appreciate it too."

"Why don't you grab some shuteye and I'll do some checking around for them two jaspers you trailed in?"

Hunter stood up. "Gotta go see the marshal first."

"Suit yourself. Key will be on the bar when you get back." Wootton poured himself another generous portion from the dusty bottle and grinned at Hunter. "Had a rough night myself."

Hunter walked the tired mustang down to the livery, paying double for an extra portion of oats and hay. The hostler shook his head, wondering why anyone would waste good money on such a shabby-looking, worn-out creature.

Hunter opened the door to the marshal's office, his step a little livelier from the potent whiskey. Right now it was the only source of energy left in him. He found a young deputy cleaning a Spenser rifle. Deputy U.S. Marshall Pat Kelly looked up from his cleaning at the trail-weary man.

"Looking for Marshal Bounds," Hunter said as he dropped into the nearest chair. "Mind if I have a cup?" Hunter asked, indicating the pot on the stove. Kelly laid the Spenser aside and fetched Hunter a cup of the black liquid, looking him over all the while.

"From the looks of it, you been riding long and hard, Mr. . . . ?"

Hunter. James Hunter." Kelly's eyes widened.

"Marshal's been expecting you . . . three or four days ago."

"Ran into a mite of trouble, son."

"Kelly's the name, sir, Pat Kelly. You just drink your coffee and I'll run fetch the marshal, although he ain't likely to be too happy for being woke up." Kelly smiled, not at all concerned. "Marshal just got back from Fort Garland. Took a prisoner down to stand trial. Been traveling all night."

"Know the feeling." Hunter had a second cup while he waited for Bounds.

U.S. Marshal Frank Bounds stomped in bleary-eyed and hatless. His thick stock of white hair lay in all directions. He had slept for only thirty minutes, and it showed. Slightly under six feet, Bounds was a tough veteran of countless gold-mining towns throughout the Rocky Mountain region. Now a shade past sixty, he commanded the whole Colorado Territory. His handshake was rock hard as he introduced himself to Hunter. Without asking, Kelly brought his superior a cup of the dark coffee before pulling up a chair for himself. Bounds settled behind his desk and Hunter wasted no time in giving him the details surrounding the two men he was after.

"And you figure them to be in Denver?"

Hunter suppressed a yawn. "They were still on the stage at the last way station. Shouldn't be too hard to find the driver, Clint Loper, and ask."

"Pat, you heard the man. Haul your tail over to the station and . . . oh, hell, you know what to do." Bounds raked his fingers through his tangled hair.

"Wan' another cup?" Hunter declined. The Taos lightning was wearing off, and his whole body felt as heavy as a sack of ore. It took great effort to keep his mind focused on business.

"Something else I need you to check. Are any of the old

98

Reynolds gang still around?"

"You thinking they carrying gold from the Buckskin Joe robbery? Hell, son, they covered that gulch with a fine-tooth comb. Even brought in Chinks to give it the once-over. And they would sift through Pikes Peak if they thought a flake of dust was lying at the bottom." Hunter was inclined to believe Buck. They had found the cache of gold, and that was that.

"Could be the others never knew about the gold." The marshal studied Hunter's wounded face for a moment, toying with that line of thought.

"That much gold would attract a lot of attention around here since the recession. A bank would have trouble keeping it quiet."

"Bankers can be bought—especially now."

"True." Bounds pulled a paper from his desk and handed it to Hunter. "Almost forgot." Hunter read the wire to Bounds from Nate Gage.

"Told him I would provide all the security I could," Bounds said. "Now that you're here, you can run the show. After all, you know more about these things than we do."

"I'll still need your help and the use of your deputies while the President is in Denver." Hunter stood up to leave.

"You can count on my office for any support you need."

As he returned to Wootton's, Hunter thought of the two men and what connection they could possibly have with the President of the United States. Nothing made sense to his fog-crowded brain. He sighed heavily as he entered the hotel. He would give Wootton a message to send to Nate. There was no way he was going to try to find the telegraph office in his condition.

CHAPTER TWENTY

They slipped into Madame Vestal's side entrance unseen. Meekam still clung to the saddlebags. Belle Siddons sat behind her polished desk sipping hot tea from an expensive gold-trimmed sky-blue china cup. There were four men present. None, however, were drinking tea.

"Come in, Mr, Meekam," Belle said politely. "Care for some excellent spiced tea?"

Meekam barely responded with a slight shake of his head. He was busy studying each of the men. Belle shrugged. She had kept her part of the agreement.

Meekam cleared his throat. "I deliberately asked Madame Vestal to provide a few good men to choose from for a special mission." Meekam looked over at Belle Siddons, who was toying with her cup. "This mission requires men with special skills and a deep love for the South."

Belle Siddons stood up. "I have a business to run, and this matter does not concern me further." She opened the door, pausing to look back at Meekam. "One more thing, Mr. Meekam, don't ever come here again," she said, and with that closed the door behind her.

Her heady smell lingered in the room, and Quirt felt the heat rise in him. He had never seen a more beautiful woman. What he wouldn't give to know her better. One thing was damn sure, he was going looking tonight, and to hell with Meekam.

Meekam continued. "It's by necessity I keep the group small. Besides myself and Tyler here, I will need three more men." None of the facial expressions on the hard-bitten men changed at this new development. They each thought they would be hired.

"Those chosen will not be allowed to turn back. Ever!" His

voice sounded like a hammer striking an anvil. One of the men stepped forward.

"Muh name's Jacob Snider, Mr. Meekam," he said with a heavy drawl. "They call me Tader fer short. Helped raise taders down in south Alabama." His handclasp was firm, and Meekam could see the resoluteness lying behind the light brown eyes. Snider was dressed in casual garb with a cheap topcoat. He had no visible weapons, yet Meekam felt sure he was armed. "I wuz a sergeant and served under Lieutenant Colonel Paul Quallebaum in the defense of Mobile. Might say I specialize in heavy artillery and explosives."

Frank Maxwell spoke without offering his hand. His voice was deep and it carried a hard edge. A low-slung holster was buckled around his narrow hips. Meekam figured him for a gambler or gunfighter . . . or both. "I was a major in the Fifth Texas Cavalry. My specialty was shooting Yanks," he said with grim humor.

"You'll get a chance to shoot some more," Meekam promised.

The third man, Billy Hamill, was a tall, stout-built fellow with a sharply angled face. He had a case-hardened appearance. Dressed in a somber black suit and flat-brimmed hat, Hamill told Meekam he had been a member of Wheat's Tigers, a group of tough, belligerent men who possessed an amazing appetite for fighting.

"Lost my brother and two cousins in 'sixty-one at Manassas. Blue-bellies called it Bull Run," Hamill said as a way of explanation. His smoky-blue eyes never wavered before Meekam. Meekam felt Hamill was not much of a talker, but what he did say he could back up.

The last fellow was a short, rat-faced individual with wet black eyes. His clothes were threadbare and smelly. Under the thin coat Meekam could see the walnut butts of two pistols and a huge knife. George "Lefty" Thompson, from the hill country of Georgia, grew up on the wrong side of the law by helping his paw make and sell whiskey to the local saloons. The seedier side of life suited him just fine.

"I joined the Seventh Infantry Regiment after my paw and brother was ambushed and killed by Yankees," Lefty said in a high-pitched whine. "Call me Lefty 'cause I was wounded in my hand." He held his right hand out for Meekam to see the scars. "Course it's all well now and I kin use it as good as ever," Lefty hurried on, seeing the look on Meekam's face. Meekam took an instant disliking to the evil-smelling little man. He appeared to have a rather weak character, and the last thing he needed was another Quirt Tyler. No doubt Lefty would sell out for the price of a beer. The decision on whom to leave behind was easy.

"Snider, Maxwell, Hamill," Meekam said, "consider your-selves hired." Then he turned to the little man. "Thompson, I'm afraid you will not do. It's not your lack of skills, God knows, everyone in this room is highly experienced. It's simply your height. I need taller men."

Thompson's face grew dark and his eyes snapped with fire. "I can take any man in this room . . . including you, Meekam." The little man seemed ready to explode. "Could slit your throat and you'd never know it!" Lefty fingered the large knife at his belt, and for a moment Quirt felt sure the little man was going to attack Meekam over the insult. Slowly he relaxed and an evil grin spread across his face.

"To hell with you and the rest of you as well." He walked to the door and paused to look back at Meekam with rodentlike eyes.

"Don't ever cross my trail, Meekam, or you just might find out how dangerous small men can be." He slammed the door behind him. No one spoke. All tough men, each cleaned out his own nest of rattlers when called to. And Lefty Thompson was as poisonous as they come. Meekam had been warned.

Meekam put Thompson's swagger from his mind and got down to business with the three remaining men. "Tomorrow morning each of you will be given five hundred dollars to spend as you wish for the next few days. The remaining two thousand will be deposited in the bank with instructions to release it only on my personal appearance. Before the close of the business day, when we make our move, I will release the money in each of your accounts for you . . . or your next of kin. Any questions?"

Billy Hamill spoke up. "What you're offering is more than

fair, and I can vouch for Snider and Maxwell. Whatever it is you want us to do, we'll ride the river with you no matter how deep it gets. When you get ready for us, come by the Gray Tavern." Hamill's unwavering eyes never left Meekam. With Hamill at his back, Meekam knew he didn't have to worry about the rest of them doing their duty. Now all he had to see to was Quirt.

CHAPTER TWENTY-ONE

"You still look like you need a week of sleep," Wootton said the next morning over breakfast. The big man was tearing at a huge plate of food. Hunter merely mumbled, sipping the hot coffee gingerly. He felt as tired as when he had gone to bed. He debated for a moment whether to ask Wootton for a small shot of lightning and thought better of it. Wootton eyed the hollow-faced Hunter as he picked at the eggs in front of him. The big man took a noisy swallow from the quart-size cup.

"Didn't find out much about the two men you trailed in," Wootton said, "except they did arrive on yesterday's stage." Hunter never figured any different. They had headed for Denver on purpose and not because of the shooting. And that thought upset him even more. He took a careless swallow of the steamy liquid and burned his tongue.

"Anything else?"

"That's about it. Where they went after that is anybody's guess. You know how it is here. People coming and a-going all the time. Two more drifters, more or less, don't make fer much excitement."

"Where would you go if you were carrying a saddlebag full of gold?"

"We don't know if he's carryin' anything more in them bags than his drawers," Wootton said dryly. "But fer argument's sake, I'll consider the question." Wootton forked the last of his food in and washed it down with coffee. Hunter forced himself to eat even though he was not hungry. His body needed the nourishment.

"If I were them, I'd deposit the stuff and get myself some greenbacks. In case you ain't noticed, flashing gold around here can be hazardous. Get your gullet slit fer the price of a beer."

104

"What then?"

"Do some hell-raising and wenching if I had been long on the trail." Hunter doubted the tall, snake-eyed one was the type to indulge no matter how long it had been. But it was a place to start.

"You might check over to Ada Lamont's on Arapaho Street. Runs the most famous place hereabouts." Wootton winked knowingly. "Ada arrived here a couple months before me and set up shop in late 'fifty-eight. She's a dark-eyed beauty still. Preacher husband run off with a lady of doubtful reputation while they was heading west. Never could figure that . . . but then, most preachers ain't toting a whole lot of smarts fer as I'm concerned. Ada moved in a shack on Indian Row, but it didn't take long business outgrew her accommodations. Now she's in a pretty two-story house over to Arapaho."

"Sounds like you know her pretty well," Hunter said with a smile.

"I admit to one er two sessions over there . . . don't need the treatment like I once did." They laughed. Wootton pulled a crumpled piece of paper from his coat pocket. "Clear forgot. You got a wire yesterday from a Nate Gage." Hunter took the wire. It had been sent from Julesburg. Gage was his usual stoic self. The wire stated "HUG" was due to arrive in Cheyenne as planned. Although Grant could have switched to the Kansas Pacific at Julesburg, he preferred to continue with his Union Pacific friends to Cheyenne and take the Denver Pacific south. The Denver Pacific was built by the citizens of Denver after they learned the Union Pacific intended to cross the Divide at Evans Pass, leaving Denver without rail service. As it stood now, three railroads served Denver.

Outside Wootton's, Hunter surveyed the early morning crowd intermingled with stragglers from the previous night's pursuits. Among the broadcloth-suited businessmen were rough-and-tumble miners and buckskin-clad individuals with silent, watchful eyes. The cloudless blue sky was intensely bright, and the feel of the sun lifted his spirits somewhat. A distant rumble over the mountains spoke of another spring storm building to the west. Moments later Hunter felt the cool mountain breeze on his face and without further thinking ambled off in toward the marshal's office. Hunter did not notice the lone figure watching him closely from the doorway of Blackwell's General Store. Once Hunter turned the corner, the man beat a hasty retreat to a run-down hotel two blocks south.

Hunter wandered over to the telegraph office to wire Colfax in Fairplay asking about Buck's condition. Afterward he paused on the steps outside to consider his next move. One thing he had to do was get on with arrangements for Grant's impending arrival, yet he knew he couldn't stop searching for the two men either . . . for Buck's sake as well as for his own.

Meekam was reading the morning paper when Quirt burst into his room loaded down with packages. He dumped them on the bed. The Texan's face was flushed with excitement.

"I saw him!" Meekam frowned, sorting through the bundles.

"Saw who?"

"The one shot Toby. The one with that old geezer you plugged back in the mountains."

"Where?" Meekam asked, his eyes suddenly alive.

"Just up Ferry Street. Didn't see me."

"You sure it was him?"

"I'm sure. Face was all scarred up. That ain't all. He's the one shot Uncle Louis back there in the Wilderness." Meekam stopped looking through the bundles and stared hard at Quirt.

"That's a little hard to swallow. After all this time. And to be here now."

"I tell you, it's him. Toby and me, neither one could forget. Hell, we musta eyed each other for five minutes at point-blank range before Uncle Louis cut loose. Explains why Toby's dead." Meekam was silent for a moment, his mind busy with the possible implications. Obviously the man had been fit enough to trail them here. He wished now he had left the old mountain coot alone. Toby wasn't worth it then or now. If what Tyler said was true, then the Yankee may have recognized Toby and Quirt as well.

"Tyler, stay away from this man," Meekam said coldly. "Nothing is going to interfere with my plans . . . understood?"

"But hell, Joe. He killed *my* brother . . . and Uncle Louis."
Quirt was pleading. "I can fix him so's it won't cause no
ruckus."

"I don't care if he gut-shot your mother. *Leave him alone!*"
Meekam pinned him with rattlesnake eyes, and Quirt could
feel the chill of his stare in the pit of his stomach. How come it
was okay for Meekam to get revenge for Billy's murder and he
had to stand by and let a man walk around free who's killed two
of his relatives? It was then Quirt made his decision. If he
could pull it off, he was going to kill the Yankee and cut loose
for Texas and to hell with Meekam and his plans. He owed Toby
that much.

The three hired gunmen crowded into the cheap hotel room
a short while later. They took notice of the new twill suits and
bowler hats Meekam and Tyler were wearing. The suit felt
uncomfortable and strange to Quirt and he didn't see why he
had to wear such a getup.

Each man left the First National Bank of Denver two hours
later better off than they had been in a very long time. It had
taken Toby's share of the gold to arrange for the special
deposits with the bank's vice president—and to buy his silence
as well. Meekam knew word of such a large deposit would leak
out within a few days, but by then it wouldn't matter. As yet
none of the hired gunmen knew what Meekam was planning.

"First thing I'm going to do is get myself a bath, new clothes,
and mix it up a little at the Palace. Then with the best whiskey
money can buy, I'm heading over to Ada's and get myself two
gals instead of one," Frank Maxwell stated. Quirt's ears perked
up.

"Who is this Ada you speaking about?" They were standing
in front of the bank, feeling good, and the three gunmen
laughed together.

"Ada Lamont," Maxwell said. "Where you been? Runs the
most famous house in these parts. Tell you what, meet me later
at the Palace and I'll see to it you're treated like royalty over to
her place. Hell, anything for a fellow Texan . . . especially if
he's totin' cash."

The gunmen drifted off, leaving Quirt and Meekam alone in
the cold sunshine. He had money, more than he ever had in his

life, but Quirt kept seeing Toby's cold rock grave. He needed to chase these thoughts away, and he wondered idly if Ada was open this early for business.

"Enjoy yourself, Tyler, it won't last long," Meekam said with a mirthless smile. "And stay away from the Yank."

Meekam strolled off without a backward glance. Quirt stared at the retreating Meekam and realized for the first time how much he really hated his cousin . . . and feared him. He ran a tongue over dry lips. What he needed was a drink. He started for the opulent Palace, his spirits rising from the bulge in his pockets.

CHAPTER TWENTY-TWO

Nate Gate threaded his way past the starched white linen-covered tables set with fine crystal and silverware in the dining car, the Delmonico, oblivious to the tantalizing smells. Single-mindedly he strode into the President's parlor car, where Grant sat discussing the railroad's westward and northern expansion routes with Grenville Dodge and Sidney Dillon. The car was resplendent in plush overstuffed chairs, rich hangings, and hand-carved inlaid mahogany paneling. A small table, around which the three men sat, held various maps and engineering drawings to which Dodge was gesturing. The President sat quietly smoking his cigar, listening to Dodge expound on the record-setting pace the Union Pacific was making through the rugged mountains of western Montana. At the same time, the stern-faced Dillon was urging Grant to extend his stay and attend several of the ceremonies being planned later in the month in Wyoming and Montana as the steel tracks cut deeper into the mountains.

Grant always had a special fondness for the West, and it would take very little persuasion for him to change his travel plans. Dillon knew just where to aim his punches.

Nate paused by the door for a moment, listening to the persuasive Dillon as Grant rolled the big cigar from side to side in his mouth. A characteristic sign Nate knew only too well. And it usually spelled trouble for him. The President looked up at his towering aide, and a barely perceptible nod from Grant told Gage all he needed to know. Nate accepted the decision calmly while his mind raced ahead with details for providing the extra security that would be needed. He hoped Hunter was in no hurry to return to his ranch.

The President held up his hand, cutting Sidney Dillon off in

109

mid-sentence. "Okay, Sidney, you've convinced me. I only hope you can do likewise with Julia. She expects me back no later than the end of this month." The Union Pacific director allowed a broad smile to crease his characteristic somber features.

"Why not send for Mrs. Grant and you both attend the opening ceremonies?"

Dodge added, "This would give you time to visit other gold camps in the territory as well." Grant liked that idea more than he liked attending the ceremonies. He never enjoyed being on public display, and he could never understand why people made such a fuss over him.

"Nathaniel, would you see to the details? No need Julia being here till the middle of the month." Nate Gage nodded his understanding of Grant's hidden meaning. The President did not want his wife out beforehand to interfere with his tour. Dillon pulled a heavy gold watch from his vest and looked at the time before snapping the lid shut again.

"Time for lunch. Anyone care to join me?" Dodge nodded and packed up his charts.

"You two go ahead," Grant said, blowing an evil-looking cloud of smoke toward the polished ceiling. "I'll be along directly." Both men nodded and left. Grant motioned Gage to one of the plush chairs. Nate sat down and laid the wire from Hunter on the small table. The President read the cryptic message.

IN PLACE STOP TAKE EXTRA CARE WITH PACK-
AGE STOP

Hunter

"Knew something was eating you when you first came in," Grant said, puffing ineffectively on the died-out cigar. Nate hoped he would not relight it.

"Hunter is concerned for your safety, Mr. President. I intend to double security as James suggests."

Grant stood up and placed the dead cigar on the table. "As always, Nathaniel, you do as you see fit. Think I'll get a little something to eat." He turned back at the door and looked at the

110

worried Nate.

"Do you think I made a wise decision about staying?" Nate Gage considered his answer carefully, not because he was afraid to offend Grant but sometimes snap decisions without careful planning had a way of changing history. Grant stood patiently by, his hand on the doorknob.

Finally Gage spoke. "Unless James has uncovered something posing a real danger that can't be dealt with, I see where the decision has certain merits. The political exposure in the western half of the country is definitely a plus and it gives legitimacy to your being in the area for so long."

Grant smiled and opened the parlor door. Gage stood up quickly.

"I'll see you to the dining car, Mr. President." Gage shifted the Starr .44 forward slightly for a faster draw.

CHAPTER TWENTY-THREE

Quirt turned up Blake Street and entered the warm recesses of the Palace, glad to be off the cold streets. He felt as if everyone were staring at him in his strange new clothes. The plush curtains were opened wide on the stage and workers were busy moving things about. He wondered when the next show would begin. The Palace was nearly empty except for a few diehards still at an all-night poker game.

Quirt ignored the few stragglers at the bar who looked him over from head to toe. He knew what they were thinking—that he was some eastern dude. It caused his anger to boil up.

"Bottle of your best whiskey," he said a little too loudly. Flustered, Quirt slapped a few greenbacks on the bar and, not bothering to collect his change, found a seat at a table with a clear view of the entrance and the bar. He took two quick shots of the smooth liquid to steady his nerves. The whiskey had none of the bite the cheap stuff had. On an early morning empty stomach, the whiskey caused his pulse to leap and a rapid flush to spread outward from his guts. He poured another drink but sipped at it slowly. Wouldn't do to get oiled this early in the day. Besides, he had another thirst to quench . . . and badly.

Lefty Thompson entered the Palace and approached the bar in the same grimy clothes of the day before. Quirt watched as the little man ordered a beer, and suddenly an idea flared like a match in his brain. It could work, Quirt thought, but he would have to be careful. This Thompson was mean and proddy to boot.

Quirt, bolstered by the fire in his veins, rose unsteadily to his feet and made his way to the bar, where Lefty stood nursing the beer, a black scowl on his face.

"Excuse me, ah—" Quirt searched for a way to begin. Lefty turned and glared hard at the Texan. He didn't recognize Quirt in the new clothes and figured him for a greenhorn easterner. "Remember me? Last night in Madame Vestal's place?" Lefty peered hard at the dude, irritated by his manner. His beady eyes lit up and then changed to hard points of red anger.

"Yeah, so what?"

"If you join me at my table," Quirt replied in his most civil tongue, "I believe we can do business together that would be mutually beneficial." Lefty stared hard at the slickly dressed man and for a moment toyed with the idea of slitting his throat because of his association with the man who had ridiculed him. He motioned for Quirt to lead the way. They sat down, and Quirt offered Lefty a shot of whiskey.

"Never touch the stuff anymore. Makes me weird, then bad things start happening." He stroked the knife handle. Quirt took a hasty gulp to focus his wits.

"Well, yes. Sorry about last night. I would never, ah, consider your height to be a problem."

"It never has!" Lefty shot back. Quirt thought it best he get to the point before the little man flew into another rage.

"Well, ah, as I was saying, I have a job requiring talents such as yours."

"What kind of job?"

"The silent kind," Quirt said evenly, his eyes straying to the man's knife. Unconsciously Lefty's hand flew to the big handle and stroked it like a high-backed cat.

"I'm listening." Quirt told him of meeting the Yankee soldier at the battle of the Wilderness, the death of his uncle and later his brother.

"Appears this gent is overdue his killing. What's your game?" Lefty asked.

"Simple. You take the Yankee out and I'll give you a hundred now and two when it's done." Lefty covered his excitement. With the depression and all, he had been forced to rolling drunks for pocket change. Hell, he would have killed the man for half that amount . . . especially a Yankee.

"Deal. How do I find this rooster?" Quirt described Hunter, including the scar on his face.

"I believe he's staying at Wootton's Hotel. Saw him coming out of there early this morning." Quirt slid the money over to Lefty. Lefty lifted his beer in silent salute and downed the contents in one gulp.

"One other thing. I get the feeling this Yankee is no slouch when it comes to fighting."

Lefty grinned, exposing yellowed teeth. "Rest easy. Job's good as done." He strode out of the Palace, feeling the flush of his newfound wealth while his mind toyed with the idea of extracting even more money from the green dude.

Quirt was startled by the made-up woman who came up behind him quietly.

"Buy a gal a drink, handsome?" she asked, flashing Quirt a false yet effective smile. Saltwater Sally, her deeply plunging neckline revealing more than enough bosom to build an instant fire in Quirt. He found himself looking between cleavage deeper than a Texas arroyo.

"Drink, hell! I'll buy you all the champagne you can hold long as you keep me happy till sunrise." The woman let out a deep, throaty laugh.

"That's a long time from now."

"Yeah, well, it's been a long time, and I don't figger on rushing things." He showed her a wad of bills, and Saltwater Sally wasted no time in escorting the willing Texan to more comfortable surroundings.

CHAPTER TWENTY-FOUR

Hunter found Marshal Bounds as he had left him the day before, disheveled and looking as if he had never gone back to bed.

"Morning, Bounds." Hunter got a cup and filled it from the stove. Bounds merely grunted as he continued to sort through a stack of Wanted posters. Hunter took a chair near the stove. He would be glad when winter released its hold on Colorado. He was ready for spring.

"I tell you, it's got to where this job is more paperwork than anything else," Bounds said, holding up a thick sheaf. "Ride this desk more than I do my horse." He shoved the pile of papers into a desk drawer and grinned perversely. "Let Kelly do it later; he needs the practice."

"You come up with anything yet?"

"Nope. If they deposited gold in this town, ain't none of the banks saying. Know it can buy a lot of silence. Got Kelly riding that angle now."

"Could be we won't ever know . . . leastwise while it counts."

"Guess Wootton told you the two men did arrive on the stage. The stage driver wasn't much help other than to say the tall one clung to them saddlebags like his life depended on it. Course they could have caught a train for the States, and you ain't never going to know it." Hunter shook his head.

"They didn't leave. Gut feeling tells me they came to Denver for a purpose other than to hide their trail."

Deputy Kelly burst through the door with the energy of a man who has yet to lose his youth and enthusiasm for living.

"No luck. Not a single bank admits to receiving any large gold deposit, although they all expressed an interest in doing so." Hunter never doubted all they were going to find for now was a dead end. Gold had a way of keeping people silent.

"Marshal, need a couple deputies to assist our men in escorting the President from Cheyenne." Bounds looked at Hunter curiously but said nothing. He was thinking, why an escort from Cheyenne?

"Like to volunteer, sir," Kelly spoke up.

"All right, Kelly, you and Sanders get your butts up there on the afternoon train. And mind your manners." Kelly grinned broadly at the prospect of a once-in-a-lifetime opportunity to meet the President of the United States. Hunter wrote a note to Nate Gage and handed it to Kelly.

"Look for the biggest and meanest-looking hombre around. You'll find him next to the President, most likely. Keep your badges in plain view. With Nate Gage you never know how he might react to two strangers waltzing up."

"Yes, sir," Kelly said, not sure if Hunter was joking or not. Hunter headed for the door, leaving Kelly to decide for himself.

"I've a meeting this afternoon with the mayor and the trade commission and God knows who else. Anything comes up, you can find me at Wootton's most likely."

Hunter spent the better part of the afternoon with local government functionaries arranging the President's schedule. Near the end of the day Hunter met Henry Teller, president of the Colorado Central Railroad. He took an instant liking to the intelligent-eyed Teller, who was making grand preparations to mark the historic event.

"If it's okay with you, I will meet the train at Black Hawk and take him up to Central City in my own personal carriage. We have yet to extend the line that far," Teller said. The frock-coated attorney sported a narrow beard along his jawline, and his stiff black hair stood in all directions.

"Don't see a problem with that, Mr. Teller, except we'll need eight horses for our security people."

"Thought of that already." Hunter found Henry Moore Teller a remarkable man. He had come to Central City in 'sixty-one as a lawyer from New York and had made his fortune by taking shares in claims and stamp mills in payment for some

116

of his legal services.

It was dusk before Hunter left the likable Teller and made his way back to Wootton's. He was dog tired and hungry but more tired of the people clamoring for an audience with the President. He disliked this part of the job the most. It was no wonder Gage pawned it off on him. Hunter smiled, feeling the scar on his jaw tighten and itch at the same time. He rubbed the spot gingerly, his mind going to Jay and Buck again as he stepped through the doors of Wootton's saloon. The strong odor of smoke, sweat, and alcohol caused his nostrils to flare sharply after breathing the sweet clean air pushing down from the mountains.

Wootton was not around, and Hunter ordered a beer while his stomach growled for food. He promised himself an early supper and bed. He looked around at the small crowd and realized Wootton had no piano. That was good. Most were out of tune anyway and usually played by someone who should have stuck to plowing. He failed to notice the little man at the end of the bar who was studying him intently. Lefty lingered over the raw scar on Hunter's face. He pretended to be slightly drunk as he watched his victim closely.

Lefty smiled, feeling the wad of bills in his pocket. After this jasper settled in for the night, he would buck the tiger at Ada's for a while. Let the Yankee get good and asleep . . . would be his last.

"Jim," Wootton bellowed across the room at Hunter as he came down the stairs leading to the hotel's rooms. Hunter pushed away from the bar and headed over to meet the burly giant, taking the half-empty glass with him.

"Where you been, son? Got a whole passel of wires fer you." They moved to the bar near Lefty, Wootton fishing in his pocket for the messages.

"Been off doing my civil duty," Hunter replied, taking the folded wires from Wootton. Lefty swayed drunkenly in their direction to catch anything he could use later.

"A mite wrinkled, but I been carryin' them around since noon." Hunter scanned the wires quickly, looking for a reply from Colfax.

"Read the one where Grant would be here tomorrow late,"

Wootton said rather sheepishly. "You gonna bring him around fer a drink of Uncle Dick's lightning, ain't you?"

"We'll see," Hunter said, not taken in at all by Wootton. Lefty's ears perked up at Grant's name, and suddenly several things slid into place. So that was Meekam's plan. He wondered how he could use this new knowledge for his own gain. If he had known this Yankee was connected to Grant, he would have asked for more money.

Hunter found the wire from Colfax. Wootton hollered for his bartender to bring them fresh beers.

"What's it say? Ol' Buck still among us?" Hunter nodded.

"One of the Jensen boys has gone back to town for more medical supplies to fight an infection. Other than that, Buck is still holding his own." Relief swept over Hunter, and he said a small prayer. Wootton slapped Hunter on the back.

"Hell, son, me and Buck has been through a sight worse than a little infection. He'll make it." Hunter only wished he could believe Wootton . . . for Jay as well as for himself. Lefty was all ears, craning his neck awkwardly to read one of the wires Hunter had placed on the bar.

"See by yore look you might be a-doubting ol' Uncle Dick," Wootton said with a bare-toothed grin as he slipped into his mountain lingo. "Recollect ol' Buck and I wuz a sight worse off in the winter of 'forty-three." Wootton's voice rose an octave or two so all those present could hear. "We wuz both a-workin' this here valley over to the Yampa and beaver wuz scarcer than gold dust in a whore's drawers, when a raidin' party of 'Rapahos caught us flatfooted a-setting traps. Ol' Buck took an arrow er two right off. Wal, sir, I wuz knee-deep in them icy waters tryin' to hide behind a limb no bigger'n yore finger, a trap in one hand an' the Henry in the other. Them 'Rapahos wuz a-headin' home and figgered to take us along." By now Wootton had every ear in the place. Long known as a storyteller of his frontier days, fighting Indians and trail-blazing with the likes of Bridger and Carson, Wootton had no equal.

"We commenced to shooting and a-stabbing and afore long things began to heat up, boys. Them 'Rapahos wuz trail hungry and hard-assed mean, and they wanted our topknots somethin' ferce. One a them Injuns had an ol' rifle and he laid a crease down Buck's topknot you coulda planted corn in. Wal, not wantin' to be left out, I took a feather in the hip. Now, as I said, we wuz doin' a respectable job on them Injuns but they wuz determined to take home more'n a sore ass. So's they come at us hot and heavy. Lordy, they wuz more feathers a-flyin' that day than in a whole flock a geese. Musta been fifteen rushed us." All card playing had suspended and even Lefty momentarily forgot Hunter at his side.

Wootton paused to empty the glass of beer, letting the tension build to a fine state. He was an old hand at working up a crowd and making it pay.

"'Bout the time I thought we wuz done fer, I looked over to ol' Buck and he wuz spoutin' blood in all directions and looked like a porkypine with all them feathers a-sticking ever which away. He looked back through them flyin' feathers and tol' me not to shoot more'n my fair share. Here wuz a man plum shot full a holes and hell-bent on enjoyin' it to the end. Wal, them 'Rapahos wuz down to five er six afore they toted up the score and decided they wanted to see what home looked like again." All was quiet for a long time.

A miner from the back of the smoky saloon finally yelled out, "Hey, Uncle Dick, did thet fellar with all them arrows make it?" Wootton shook his shaggy head sadly as if indicating otherwise . . . then a knowing grin.

"Hell, yes, but I didn't!" Wootton roared louder than anybody. Even Hunter felt better. They took no notice of Lefty as he exited under the roar of laughter.

Marshal Bounds joined them over dinner at Ma Hawkins's. The eatery had become the most famous restaurant this side of the Continental Divide. She had come west with her husband, Deacon Hawkins, in 'sixty-two, from the fertile valley of Ohio. Like so many others, he had caught the fever from reading dime novels and newspaper accounts by journalists eager to sell papers. What Deacon Hawkins found, like others late to the diggings, was that camp life was hard, prices exorbitant, and all the paying claims taken. While her husband turned to drink and cards for solace, Helen Hawkins turned to the only thing she knew to keep body and soul alive. When Deacon was killed over a card game, her business seemed to triple, and now she drew crowds from all over the Pikes Peak mining district.

Wootton tore at a piece of flaky apple pie three times normal size. Hunter still could not bring himself to try the pastry. He wanted nothing to compare with Jay's cooking, yet he wondered if he would ever have the opportunity to taste it again. He put his mind back on the business at hand.

"The President is in Cheyenne," he informed the marshal. The other wire Wootton had given him had been from Nate saying "HUG" would depart Cheyenne the following afternoon.

"Glad to hear it. Means Kelly and Sanders won't have much time for trouble-making," Bounds responded.

"I'm afraid they will find life a little hard with Nate Gage around. He still considers eating and sleeping luxuries not to be abused."

This brought Bounds to the question nagging him all day. "You expecting trouble I don't know about?" He watched Hunter closely for a reaction.

"Playing a hunch for now, Marshal. Rather not say if there is a clear and present danger to the President until I learn more."

Bounds shrugged his shoulders. "Change your mind, you know where to find me. After all, I am a federal marshal, and his safety is my concern as well."

"I'll remember that. Didn't mean to give you the impression I was cutting you out of the action. Believe me, I will come running at the first sign of trouble."

Bounds wiped a crumb of pie from his mouth. "You asked me about the Reynolds gang yesterday." Wootton looked sharply at Bounds. "What is known is pretty much public knowledge. Jim Reynolds and his gang, at least all but two, were killed while trying to escape," Bounds said dryly. He and Wootton exchanged glances. "According to a former deputy of mine, Mark Kellerman, who worked as a guard for the old Phillips mine near Buckskin Joe, they trailed the two men for two days before losing them. Indications were they headed into New Mexico. The rest of the gang were later shot when they tried to escape as they were being transferred to Fort Lyon.

Trail seems to end there as far as the Reynolds gang goes."

"And nothing ever known of the two fled to New Mexico?"

"Disappeared, for all anybody knows." Bounds got up to refill his cup. Hunter toyed with several ideas. The two he was after had been in the same area the Reynolds gang had frequented. They obviously found gold, from what Buck said. The thing that bothered Hunter was why wait nearly ten years to reclaim the gold? Why not wait a few months, or possibly a year even, but ten! And where did the President fit in? Something just wasn't right. Hunter wasn't thinking too clearly. What he needed was sleep in the worst way.

Later, after a nightcap with Wootton, Hunter tossed about on the bed unable to sleep. Troubled by the unanswered questions floating in his head, he lay listening to the sounds of laughter down below and was again thankful Wootton didn't have a piano. He put the pillow over his head to shut out the sounds.

After leaving Wootton's saloon, Lefty Thompson considered his next move. He had gone there looking to learn a little about his victim, but through sheer luck he had found out everything he needed to know about the man. Even the room number had been penciled on one of the wires he managed to scan. He had figured a few days to learn what he now knew in a single hour. No use waiting. Tonight would be as good as any. Later tonight, when a person was in his deepest sleep, he would let the big knife do its work. Right now he felt like a couple hands of poker at the Gray . . . and then on to Ada's.

Seventy miles away, Kelly and his partner, Sanders, were having anything but a night on the town. Nate Gage had wasted few words on the pair of lawmen and had put them to work on crowd control. They were both disappointed at not having been introduced to the President, at least. Outside of an occasional stony stare from Gage, they were completely ignored. One thing they were both glad of—they worked for Bounds and not the icy-eyed Gage.

121

CHAPTER TWENTY-FIVE

It was well past midnight before Denver settled into its customary soft murmur. Only the hard-eyed gamblers and patrons who were either drunk or fancied themselves good enough to take on the professionals were still at the tables. The normally busy streets had a light sprinkling of foot traffic, mostly diehards stumbling from one saloon to another.

The air was sharp and clear under a pale moon as Lefty cautiously made his way through the darkened alleyways, avoiding the gaslit streets altogether. He made it to the back of Wootton's without being detected.

For a moment he stood in the long shadows near the rear door of the building, recalling the soft places he had just been. The smell of her was still strong in his nostrils, but his head was clear and his heart was cold . . . for he intended to kill again.

Silently Lefty raised a rear window and eased inside. He stood for a moment to let his eyes adjust to the darkened room. Gradually he began to make out crates and sacks stacked along the walls, and realized he was standing in Wootton's storeroom. His luck was still holding, for just outside the storeroom door were the stairs leading to the rooms above the saloon. He could hear the low voices coming from the saloon and an occasional chair scrape as someone stood up or sat down. He cracked the door and peered out. This area of the hotel was empty and he slipped out of the room soundlessly. He had removed his boots in the storeroom, and his feet made little noise on the wooden stairs.

Gingerly he tried the doorknob leading into the Yankee's room and surprised to find it unlocked. His luck was really rolling now. He held his breath as he opened the door enough to slip inside. He gripped the big knife in an iron fist, his whole body tensed for an attack. He sensed the presence of the man and Lefty smiled in the darkness. With luck the job would be over before the Yankee felt the cold steel at his throat. Then he could return to the softness of the dark-eyed beauty with the sparkling laugh and gold-flecked eyes.

The nightmare came suddenly, without warning. The giant, evil-smelling beast emerged from the blackness to seize Hunter with its powerful jaws. Caught between a dreamlike state of semi-consciousness and reality, a few terrifying moments passed before Hunter was forced awake, a silent scream forming on his lips. He was drenched with sweat and his heart pounded hard against his rib cage. The stench of the grizzly was everywhere. He went downstairs for a pitcher of water to bathe his hot face. It was a long time before he felt like lying down again and even longer before he drifted into an uneasy sleep.

A warning flashed in Hunter's brain at the same time his senses were accepting the faint fragrance of perfume of wildflowers as belonging to Jay. He came fully awake, unmoving. The smell of the wildflowers persisted, and a few feet away he heard the faint whisper of cloth on bare wood. Hunter forced himself to breathe steadily, as if still asleep, while his mind focused on the intruder in his room.

Lefty listened to the steady, rhythmic breathing of the Yankee. In the dim light filtering through the window he could just make out the sleeping form of the man. Slowly he eased across the room, mindful of unseen objects. A few more steps and it would be all over for the rebel killer.

At that same instant Lefty made his lightning-quick strike, Hunter was no longer there. The downward vicious sweep of the razor-sharp bowie was meant to be a lethal blow, but the slashing knife cut through thin air. Lefty was momentarily dumbfounded. Had he misjudged the angle in the semi-darkness that badly?

Galvanized into action, Hunter felt the rush of air pass by him as he rolled to the floor, bringing his Colt from beneath his pillow with him. As he brought the gun to full cock, he heard the muffled curse, and a shadowy figure loomed over him.

Hunter fired instantly . . . once and then twice. The figure let out a strangled cry and crashed backward into the washstand. The sounds of a body hitting the floor amid breaking glass and wood told Hunter all he needed to know.

Hunter rolled to a far corner and waited for the sounds of further movement. He could hear the man's ragged breathing and he knew at least one of his slugs had been a lung shot. Somewhere below he heard a door slam and someone shouted.

Cautiously Hunter moved to the window and pushed aside the curtains for more light. He could see the intruder sprawled among the wreckage of the washstand. He found the lamp and lit it and with cocked gun he eased over to the man. The unshaven face looked back at Hunter with rodent eyes. Hunter caught the faint scent of wildflowers mixed with blood. The face was pale and drawn and blood seeped from a corner of his mouth. A large crimson circle spread slowly outward from a chest wound. The other slug had hit the man in his knife hand and traveled upward to lodge in his chest cavity. Lefty coughed and brought up a wad of bloody sputum.

"Never figgered no Yankee eastern dude could take me," Lefty said weakly.

"What makes you think I'm from the east?"

"Hell, you work for Grant, don't you?" Hunter was stunned.

"How did you know that? Who are you?" Heavy-booted men ran down the hallway and banged on the door.

"Jim, you okay?" Wootton thundered. Hunter circled the prostrate figure and let Wootton in.

"Having a party?" Wootton asked mildly, taking in the bloody scene.

"Jasper tried to knife me." Hunter bent down and picked up the bowie.

"Bring the lamp closer and let's have a look at this brave fellar," Wootton ordered. Wootton looked like a giant wild thing with his shaggy hair pointing in all directions. He had on an ugly washed-out red robe and in one big hand he carried a Greener like a toothpick. Hunter wanted to laugh in spite of the situation. Wootton's eyes narrowed as he studied the dying man's features in the lamplight.

"Howdy, Wootton," Lefty managed gruffly.

"Thompson! What in hell come over you. Figgered yore kind along with them other southern trash you hang around wasn't brave enough to pull something like this." For an instant Lefty was his old self and his eyes blazed pure hatred.

"Go to hell, Wootton. Know I'm done fer."

Hunter cut in. "Who hired you to kill me? And how did you know I worked for the President?" Lefty managed a half-smile filled with pain.

"Bet you would, Yank." His voice trailed off to a whisper and his breathing became shallow and labored. "I may be out of the game, but the party is far from being over," he whispered. His eyes flew open wide for an instant and his body went slack.

"Denver's rid of another lowlife," Wootton commented. Hunter looked pale and worried.

"Come on, Jim, looks like you could use a shot of Taos." Wootton told one of the gawkers at the door to fetch the sheriff and Skeeter Henderson, the undertaker. Hunter threw on a shirt, stuck his Colt in his pants, and followed Wootton downstairs. There would be no further sleep tonight for him.

They sat before the fire nursing coffee heavily laced with Taos lightning.

"Forgot to relock my door. Grizzly paid me another visit and I came down for a pitcher of water."

"No mind," Wootton said with a wave of his hand. "He would've found a way inside. Reckon how he linked you to General Grant?" Hunter had been thinking the same thing.

"It's more than just wanting me dead. I'm not forgetting the two who shot Buck may have had something to do with this. For revenge maybe. But gut feeling tells me the President is their objective and I'm just in their way."

Wootton took a long swallow from the cup and pulled the old robe around his ample middle. "Wal, 'ppears to me if'n they got rid of you that would take care of worryin' 'bout their back trail and leave a free hand for Grant . . . if that's they game."

"You mentioned a group of southerners this Thompson hung around with. Where can I find them?"

"Lefty? Nah," Wootton said, pouring another slug of Taos into his cup. He left out the coffee this time. "Lefty was a loner. Too mean when drunk, which was most of the time, to have any friends. He hung around the Gray Tavern, a place noted for those still carryin' a torch for the Confederate cause. But you be careful if you go there. Could be whoever hired Lefty holes up there and you might not be so lucky the next time."

"Beats losing sleep every night. Might tip their hand if I show up."

"Then you will be needin' a guide to find the place."

"Couldn't do that. Last time someone helped me, he wound up getting shot, but thanks."

The sheriff came down the stairs. "Found nearly a hundred dollars on him. Whoever paid to have you killed musta set store by your abilities. Going rate nowdays ain't but seventy-five." Hunter was not cheered by this bit of news. Moments later Skeeter Henderson came down the stairs with the body slung between two enlisted men and disappeared into the night.

Hunter got up for more coffee and Taos as the old clock above the bar chimed three times.

"Anyway, the telegrapher is loose with other people's messages?"

"Jenkins? Nah. Been knowing him fer ten years. A family man and deacon and as tight-lipped as they come about business." Hunter was glad he had sent the extra deputies as escort now. He needed to wire Nate.

Wootton had Jenkins awakened and brought over to the saloon. Disheveled and red-eyed, Jenkins took Hunter's message.

"Won't do any good," he said, rubbing sleep from his eyes, "less Luke decided to sleep over to the office, which he does sometimes when he gets a snootful and don't want to go home to his wife. If he ain't there, can't send it till six."

"Do the best you can, Mr. Jenkins," Hunter said, "and remember, it's urgent Nate Gage gets this message as soon as humanly possible." Jenkins left fired up.

The more Wootton drank, the more he slipped into past memories of his early trapping days. Hunter listened to the old mountain man, and it helped him to relax a little.

"Yessir, them wuz shinin' times," Wootton recalled. "Had a high time with the likes of Mears, Beckwourth, and old Vaskiss. Even ol' Buck Sawtelle at a few of them ronnyvoos." Wootton packed his pipe as he warmed up to his favorite subject.

"Now, Beckwourth wuz noted as a great storyteller and reputed to be one of the finest liars ever produced by the Rocky Mountain region. Truth is, I taught him all he ever knew about the subject." Wootton blew out a blue cloud of smoke and the smile faded slowly from his weathered face. "Sure do miss them boys and the hell-raisin' ronnyvoos, the likes you will never see again," he said sadly, then his face sobered.

"Tell you, Jim, and you the first to know. Sellin' out this year and headin' back down to New Mexico. Been thinkin' 'bout it fer two years er more. City is jest too big fer me, besides, life here is done dried out. Back in 'fifty-nine and 'sixty it took men like myself and Charlie Harrison and Jack O'Neil to stomp out a place fer all the others to follow. Take ol' Jack. Watched him die in the arms of Salt Lake Kate. Dry-gulched by a fellar named Rooker, a-standin' right over there in my front door. Yessir, O'Neil was a gentleman to the end."

"Why New Mexico?" Hunter asked, his troubles temporarily forgotten. Wootton's features brightened and his eyes twinkled.

"Gonna build me a toll road cross Raton Pass. If'n Otto can do it, figger I can. Kinda quiet up there. Gettin' too long in the tooth fer the city." Wootton, like other trailblazers of his day, part Indian and part cougar, would always be called back to the rocky wilds of the high mountains.

Suddenly Wootton sat up straight in his chair. "Knowed somethin' was sticking in my craw. Jest couldn't pull it out till now."

"What is it?"

"Lefty Thompson. He was in here last night. Standing next to us at the bar." Wootton's hard eyes were on Hunter. "Never paid him no mind till now. Probably heard me mention Grant to you." Wootton looked sheepish. "Sorry, Jim. Let my mouth get the best of me sometimes."

"Not your fault. He would have found out some other way. The most important thing is I stopped him."

127

Just before daylight, Byers, editor of the *News*, showed up and reluctantly Hunter filled him in on the details.

Later, as light came to the city, Hunter braved the sharp chill to walk the quiet streets, brooding about another old mountain man also getting long in the tooth. He prayed Buck was still alive. His walk carried him down to the South Platte and in the distance he could see the formidable, snow-covered Pikes Peak as the early morning sun touched its mighty crest. A timeless sentinel to those crossing the prairie. The scene lifted his spirits and gave him cause for new hope. Today the President was coming to Denver and he had yet to meet with the territorial governor.

He sighed deeply and turned his back to the sharp wind blowing down from the mountains to the west. He headed back to Wootton's and breakfast. Tonight he intended to pay a visit to the Gray Tavern and see for himself the type of polecats that hung out there.

CHAPTER TWENTY-SIX

At mid-morning Quirt returned to the seedy hotel room. After the high-priced booze and the all-night attentions of a girl named Rose, he was in need of sleep. Funny how all the girls he had known seemed to be named after flowers. He laughed to himself and lay back across the bed, tired but happy. He hoped Lefty had been as successful as he had been.

He woke later to a pounding at his door, and for a sleep-confused moment he thought the Yankee had come to kill him. He staggered to the door to find Meekam standing there, clean-shaven and clear-eyed. Obviously he had spent the night sleeping.

"Get yourself together and meet me downstairs in thirty minutes," he said coldly. Before Quirt could manage a reply, Meekam disappeared into his room, slamming the door shut behind. Quirt slammed his shut as well, exasperated. Now, what in hell was eating him, Quirt wondered.

Quirt managed to shave, using the cold water in the basin. He straightened his new clothes as best he could and went downstairs. Meekam was sitting near the door reading a newspaper, his face looking like chiseled stone. He rose to his feet, snapped the paper under his arm, and led the way outside. Quirt followed like an obedient dog. Meekam paused on the boardwalk and lit a thin black cigar.

"Eaten yet?" Meekam asked.

"Not hungry," Quirt replied, feeling his stomach quiver at the mention of food. What he really needed was a drink to steady his nerves and quiet the thunderstorm building in his midsection.

"Always figgered a man about to die oughta go on a full stomach," Meekam said casually.

129

"What—what are you talking about?" Quirt's heart leapt into his throat.

"This!" Meekam hit Quirt in the chest with the folded paper. "You can read?" Quirt took a step backward, holding on to the paper.

Hurriedly Quirt scanned the front page of the *News*, searching for whatever was making Meekam act like a wild man. Then he saw it, halfway down the page.

ATTEMPT MADE ON PRESIDENTIAL AIDE'S LIFE

Quirt quickly read the article, his heart pounding hard. The article stated that James Hunter, aide to the President of the United States, was attacked early this morning by Lefty Thompson, a known ruffian and Southern sympathizer. Thompson was subsequently shot by Hunter. Authorities believe Thompson was a paid assassin and an active investigation is under way. Quirt tried to swallow, his mouth drier than a desert-baked ball of spit. The article was followed by a scathing editorial by Editor Byers and the black mark all Denverites were made to suffer by this incident.

"Joe, I—I didn't know he was connected to *him*," Quirt pleaded. Meekam's face was flat and expressionless, a cold fury dancing behind his eyes. The boardwalk was crowded with people who looked curiously at the two men. Meekam shoved Quirt down an alleyway for about fifty yards before he spun him around.

"I ought to kill you now!" Meekam hissed. "I warned you to leave the Yankee alone. Not only is the element of surprise lost, I now have to change my plans."

"Sorry, Joe, I mean it. Toby was my own flesh and blood, your cousin, for crissakes. How was I to know this Yank was in bed with Grant?"

"The only reason you are still breathing." Quirt lowered his eyes under Meekam's onslaught. God, how he needed a drink.

"I'll do whatever you say . . . swear on Toby's grave."

"You damn right you will!" Meekam looked down at his humbled cousin with undisguised contempt. He knew the man was not reliable under pressure and wished now he had cut him loose after Toby's death.

Quirt lifted his eyes to look at Meekam and with surprising courage said, "What if the Yankee had been the one killed Billy instead of Toby. Would it made a difference?" Meekam knew Quirt was right. After all, look at him now, still trying to settle Billy's death some ten years later.

Meekam let out a long breath. "I concede the point. But don't you move outside your room except to eat and visit the outhouse. Even then you better hold it till you're ready to pop."

Meekam paused outside the hotel entrance. "I'm taking the train up to Black Hawk; see to it you stay put." After Meekam left, Quirt went up to his room and put his old clothes back on. If he was to hang around the room all day, he figured he may as well be comfortable. He thought of the Yankee. Damn Lefty's hide! Should have known not to send a pint-size man for such a job. It was that damn bottle of smooth whiskey got him to thinking such thoughts. His mouth was cotton dry and he thought of how good a cold beer would be right now. Before he realized it, he was out the door and heading for the Palace. Have a couple cold ones and get a bottle or two to sip back in the room. Help kill time, the way he figured.

Quirt killed the two beers quickly and ordered two bottles of whiskey, the cheap kind. He made a hasty sandwich from the bar as he waited. He paid for the whiskey from his dwindling money supply, regretting now the money he had given Lefty. At least no one could tie him to the attempted murder, except through Lefty . . . and Lefty was dead.

CHAPTER TWENTY-SEVEN

During breakfast Marshal Bounds dropped by as Wootton and Hunter were finishing their coffee.

"Heard about the fracas. Anything I can do?"

"Could use another couple deputies to handle the crowd once the President arrives."

"No problem. Know several good men I use from time to time."

"I've been doing some thinking about the two members of the Reynolds gang who escaped to New Mexico. Check with your marshal friends down there and give them the descriptions of the two I been trailing and see if they come up with anything.

"You figure they're the same ones chased out of Colorado ten years ago?" Bounds asked. Hunter nodded.

"Now, if'n that wuz true, how come they waited all these years to come fer the gold?" Wootton wanted to know. Bounds nodded in agreement.

"Because"—Hunter looked at the two men—"they've been in prison." Bounds's face lit up.

"You may just have something there and I know just who to contact. But that still don't mean they have any gold."

"Hell, Frank, I done told him that," Wootton said.

"True," Hunter conceded, "but I do believe Buck. And the stationmaster at Tarryall Creek said he clung to those bags like his life depended on it. And to me that spells gold."

"Can't argue there," Bounds said over his coffee.

"And it leads me to believe the two I've been trailing spotted me around town, and the Texan with the one he called Joe hired Lefty to kill me." Both Bounds and Wootton looked puzzled over this bit of news.

"Why do you think that?" Bounds asked.

"It goes back a lot of years . . . to Virginia."

"You lost me there," Bounds said.

"Bear with me. Done some thinking on this since last night and I think I'm right. It all started eleven years ago in a battle at the Wilderness and picked up again with the dead man in the canyon. Toby, the one who tried to dry-gulch me, was one of the three men I had the run-in with at the Wilderness. I'm certain the stocky one is the other. I killed the third Confederate during the skirmish."

"You saying this attempt last night was for revenge from eleven years ago and not because of your connection with Grant?" Bounds asked.

"Yes and no. If I'm dead, that clears it for Toby and at the same time gets me out of the way where the President is concerned."

"You saying they intend to assassinate President Grant?" Bounds asked in a shocked voice.

"I have only Lefty's dying words, but I think that is exactly what they're planning. Wootton heard him make the comment." The old trapper nodded his head in agreement.

"Fer shore it ain't over, like James says. Lefty wasn't noted for keeping secrets."

"If that's true," Bounds whispered, "hadn't we better let the army in on this?"

Hunter shook his head. "President Grant dislikes the simple precautions we take as it is . . . and what if I'm wrong? It would cause the President considerable embarrassment."

"Then what are you suggesting?" Bounds demanded.

"Nothing more than is already planned, at least for the moment."

"Well, better get cracking," Bounds said, standing up. "I hear anything from New Mexico, I'll be back." They watched him leave.

"Bounds is a fine man, Jim. He'll do his part and then some."

"Only hope I can do mine. Still got to convince a case-hardened hombre name of Nate Gage." There was one other long shot he had not tried, and all it would cost was the price of

133

a telegram.

As if reading Hunter's thoughts, Jenkins hurried in with an answer to his wire from Gage.

"Mr. Hunter, I am sorry for the delay. Seems Luke passed out halfway through the wingding they had for the President last night, and well . . ." Hunter took the wire.

HUG UNDER SPECIAL CARE AS ADVISED STOP
ARRIVING LATE AFTERNOON TRAIN STOP
Gage

"Will there be a reply, Mr. Hunter?"

"No, Mr. Jenkins," Hunter said, reaching for pencil and paper, "at least not to this wire. I want you to get this to army headquarters in Washington, D.C. And mark it urgent." Hunter handed the telegrapher a double eagle. "And take the missus out to dinner. I thank you, and the President thanks you." Hunter checked his watch. It was ten-thirty. He had to get going. He was scheduled to see the mayor and the territorial governor and he had promised to drop by Byers's office and let him know when the President would be arriving.

"Remind Byers of our poker game tonight," Wootton said as Hunter stood up to leave. "He still owes me rent money."

"He does?" Wootton roared with laughter.

"Private joke. Let him set up his newspaper business in a room above the saloon back in 'fifty-nine. Think he got tired of dodgin' stray bullets and moved not long after. Let's see, first paper came out on April 23, 1859 . . . got a copy 'round here someplace."

Two streets away Hunter spotted a vaguely familiar figure coming out of a saloon with two bottles of whiskey in one hand and holding a half-eaten sandwich in the other. He watched as the man crossed the street and looked his way. It was the Texan! Hunter started toward the man without thinking. All he could see was Buck's bloody body sprawled in the rocks. The Texan was a full block away and Hunter had to trot to keep him in his sights through the crowded streets. He saw the man turn down a side street while looking furtively behind him. His first impulse was to rush the Texan and shoot it out if necessary, but after cooling down a bit he realized the man may lead him back to the other one. With the Texan out of sight, Hunter broke into a run, ignoring the looks all around him. The street led to a seedier part of town. Hunter cut his pace in half when he reached the side street, which was less crowded, and he feared the Texan might spot him.

Scurrying along, Quirt felt like a bug under a microscope. He crossed the rutted streets, oblivious to the mud. Maybe it was all those lonely years herding cattle in the cedar brakes under a hot, dusty sun that allowed him to develop his sixth sense. Whatever the reason, it came into play now. He was being followed. The feeling was too strong to ignore. Quirt cast a quick glance back but didn't see a familiar face in the crowd. Someone was there and he stifled the urge to run. Damn! He wished he had done as Meekam had said.

Hunter watched as the Texan left Wynkoop and turned down F Street. The street was crowded once more and heavy freight wagons lumbered by. They were in the part of town that was nothing more than shabby saloons and crib houses.

Hunter turned the corner and stopped in his tracks. The Texan was nowhere in sight. He looked in both directions, cursing under his breath for not playing it a little closer.

From the crowded saloon Quirt watched through one of the dingy windows as a man hurried around the corner and stopped to look around. Quirt's blood froze. It was the Yankee, James Hunter. Despite the cold, Quirt broke out into a cold sweat. What if he had gone directly to the hotel? He would have been trapped for sure. Quirt looked around him in the saloon for an escape route in case Hunter decided to check the place. When he looked back, Hunter was gone.

Wildly Quirt looked up and down the street for Hunter. His chest felt ready to explode from the tension. Someone touched his arm and he nearly dropped the bottles of whiskey.

"Take it easy, honey," a soft voice purred. "Violet ain't gonna bite you, leastways where it'll show." Quirt fought to control his runaway heart as he turned to look into a homely-faced girl garishly painted and perfumed to high heaven. Her red dress trimmed with fake fur was cut low at the bodice. Her breasts were huge, and in spite of his predicament, Quirt felt a deep stirring. What he needed was a place to hide for a while, and she was just the ticket.

"You got a room?" Quirt pressed the remainder of his money into her hand as he stared hard at her heaving bosom.

"Just my type," the soiled dove replied as she leaned into him so he could feel what he had been staring at. "Direct and to the point."

Hunter waited for fifteen minutes on the corner of the street before he finally conceded the Texan must have seen him. Too many cribs and saloons to check to do any good. He had to face it—his man had escaped.

Reluctantly Hunter retraced his steps. At least he had learned one important thing. The pair was still in town. Both good and bad.

Several hours later Quirt slipped unobtrusively out the rear of the saloon and made his way back to his hotel. This time he made sure nobody followed him.

CHAPTER TWENTY-EIGHT

While the presidential entourage made its way south toward Denver, a lone figure rode the Colorado Central to Black Hawk, carefully noting the times, grades, and passes in a small notebook.

Meekam was forced to consider an alternative plan to the one he had been working on because of the Hunter affair, and as the train pulled hard to make a grade, a new idea came to him, one that was sure to be more successful than his original. He wished he had known about the physical features of this area before. It would have made his planning a lot easier. It just might turn out Quirt had done him a favor after all.

Meekam boarded the Colorado Central stage at Black Hawk for the short but rough ride up the canyon to Central City. He continued to make copious notes of the geographical features along the way. The last leg to Central City had yet to be built, as it required at least three miles of track in a grand series of switchbacks to overcome the difference in elevation.

Unlike Black Hawk, Meekam found Central City confined to a narrow canyon and buildings were by necessity crowded close together. The town was bustling with activity and the ground constantly rumbled from the heavy ore wagons. Wagoneers and pack trains jostling for room on the narrow thoroughfare filled the streets with shouts and whistles. Meekam walked the crowded streets, familiarizing himself with the place. If he chose Central City, he didn't want his plans to fail because of some dead-end alleyway. He located the imposing Teller House and spent time probing the streets and alleys leading to and around the building. Meekam knew from the newspapers that Grant was to visit the place. Even said in the article that silver bars would be laid for Grant to walk across. And all Billy ever got was a bullet in the gut. Meekam smiled coldly. If he had his way, Grant would be facedown in the dirt before he got the chance to walk across something as precious as silver.

Meekam bought a copy of the *Daily Miner's Register* and retired to a nearby saloon for a cold beer as he scanned the paper and the news of the President's impending arrival to this city.

Hunter took a streetcar to the territorial governor and military headquarters on Larimer and Fifth streets after leaving Byers's office.

"Come in, Mr. Hunter," Governor John Routt said, extending his hand. He studied Hunter warmly with piercing gray eyes. "Been expecting you. Please, sit down." Routt's voice was soft and friendly. A squarely built veteran of the union siege of Vicksburg, Hunter could see why Grant had named him to fill the position after Governor Edward McCook was dismissed for lining his pockets with Indian annuity contracts to supply beef, blankets, and other goods to the Ute, Arapaho, and Cheyenne. If his memory served him, Hunter recalled McCook bought cattle for $7.50 a head and sold them to the government for $35. Not a bad deal . . . if you didn't get caught. He was also present to witness the pain Grant suffered when he found out his Secretary of War, William Belknap, was indicted in the scandal as well and was subsequently impeached and tried for selling these annuity contracts to his friends.

This time Grant had taken no chances, so he appointed a military man he knew well and who he was sure would work scrupulously for the betterment of Colorado.

"It's a pleasure to meet you, Governor Routt," Hunter said, taking the offered chair.

"Not governor yet, Mr. Hunter," Routt said with a twinkle in his eyes. "But if I have my way with Ulysses, he will return to Washington with a recommendation to grant statehood to Colorado."

"I'm sure it's only a matter of time," Hunter replied.

"Understand you have a ranch down in Ute country? Kinda touchy living, isn't it, even with the Brunot Treaty?"

"I understand why the Ute feel the way they do," Hunter replied. "Prettiest country you will find anywhere. If I were the Ute, I'd be hard pressed to give it up too. But the sad fact is, there is no simple way to keep gold-hungry miners out of Ute territory, so we keep making treaties when and where it suits us."

"Understand how you feel, son. How did you convince the Utes to let you stay?"

"When I worked in Washington, I offered my services on behalf of the President to Otto Mears and Chief Ouray. I kept listening to Mears describe this country, and it wasn't long I was pining for the Rockies as bad as Otto wanted to get back. One thing led to another and I took Chief Ouray up on his offer to buy enough land to start a ranch."

"Can't say as I blame you. The Gunnison is beautiful country and Otto is a one-man crusade for Colorado and has been instrumental in keeping peace with the Utes. Now that you are down there, might just call on you for help if the time comes."

"Fair enough. But your best bet is still Mears or Wootton." His secretary brought in afternoon coffee, and Routt dumped three helpings of sugar into his cup. Hunter took his black.

"Bitten by the fever yet?" Routt asked as he sipped the hot liquid.

"Not so it shows. Rather spend my days in the open sunshine with a good horse under me than crawling around in some dark hole scratching at rocks."

"Know the feeling. Well, I know you're busy seeing to the needs of the President. Suppose we get down to details, and I won't keep you any longer than necessary." They agreed Routt would meet the President upon his arrival at Union Depot with a full military band followed by a tour of the city with the mayor and other functionaries. A dinner would be given later that evening with everybody that was somebody attending, something Grant rarely found enjoyable but nevertheless tolerated because of political necessity.

Back on the streets, Hunter pulled his coat tightly around

him, feeling the sharp, cutting wind whip through the muddy streets. A deep restlessness was building within him . . . for Jay and the Gunnison country. Damn, but he would be glad when Gage made it in! He needed to bounce a few ideas off him. Hunter quickened his steps toward City Hall after looking at his watch. Another hour and the President would be arriving.

"This is how we are going to do it," Gage said for the benefit of the deputy marshals. His men, bored with the familiar routine, remained alert to field any questions Gage had a mind to throw at them when they least expected it. One never took chances with Nate Gage. They were all standing in the security car, a rare treat since Gage usually insisted on one agent with the President at all times.

"As soon as the train stops, Tolin and Adams here will exit at opposite ends of the presidential car and start working the crowd." At the mention of their names, the two agents feigned interest. Thomas Tolin was a tall, lanky, open-faced individual who kept a constant smile. Like the rest of Grant's men, he, too, was a veteran of the war, serving behind Confederate lines as a valuable spy under the direction of Major Allen. Ben Adams was just the opposite. A short, thickset man with dark features, Adams served under Grant as an explosives expert, blowing strategic bridges, railroad trestles, and generally creating as much trouble as he could behind enemy lines.

"This is where I want you and your friend to step off the train in front of Jackson," Gage continued. The somber-faced Al Jackson looked calmly at the two deputies as if they were getting a tea order straight. Jackson puffed lightly on a cigar, studying the two men. His close-cropped beard and black suit made him a dead ringer for Grant at a distance. This resemblance had been utilized in the past by Gage when Jackson acted as a stand-in for Grant. Today warranted the use of the ruse once more.

"Once Jackson is off the train, the President and I will exit a few seconds later." Gage looked at the two deputies closely to see if they were following what he said. "When we start out, you two stand on either side of the President. And for God's

140

sake, keep your eyes on the crowd, *not* on the President." The two deputies nodded their understanding quickly, not wanting to rile Gage. From what they had learned from his colleagues, Nate Gage could be living hell on wheels.

"Another thing, since you both know the local dignitaries, keep your eyes peeled for anyone that don't belong. Understood?" Again both nodded their heads mutely. Gage studied them for a moment, then lit a fresh cigar.

"Good," he growled. "Let's get back to the President. We have a half hour exactly." No one questioned the time.

At the same time the President arrived at Union Depot, Meekam boarded the stage for the trip back down the canyon to Black Hawk and the eastbound train to Denver. Consequently he missed the important premature roar from the crowd as Al Jackson paused momentarily on the top steps of the platform.

Bouncing down the rocky, hard-packed road, Meekam had a deep-seated feeling Hunter might turn out to be the major obstacle to his getting to Grant. Hunter was not some eastern tenderfoot, as Lefty Thompson had obviously found out.

For now the best course of action was no action. Let them wait and worry. And when they were worn down by the constant vigil, he would make his move. Meekam smiled coldly as the afternoon light faded from the narrow canyon walls. His smile thinned out as young Billy's face floated across the soft shadows. Meekam's face softened for a moment and then hardened into a tough resolve.

"It won't be long now, Billy," Meekam whispered to the fading vision. The coach rattled into Black Hawk as twilight settled in.

CHAPTER TWENTY-NINE

A full minute slipped by before Grant felt the familiar nudge from behind and he stepped onto the platform and the waiting crowd. He disliked using a double even for a short time, and he allowed Gage the use of such ruses only on special and infrequent occasions.

The roar from the crowd was thunderous upon Grant's appearance, and in rare form he waved his hat vigorously in the late afternoon air.

Nate Gage scanned the boisterous crowd with practiced eyes for anyone exhibiting a subtle difference from those around him. He looked down on the familiar shoulders of James Hunter, who stood casually facing the crowd with the walnut butt of his Colt exposed from beneath his dress coat. Nate's rock-hard features softened for a moment. He and Hunter had been through a lot together over the years, and it felt good to have him here now. Gage caught the almost imperceptible nod the President gave to Hunter as he descended the steps to take John Routt's outstretched hand.

It was nearly two in the morning before the President sought his bed. His door was guarded by Tolin and Pat Kelly. The second watch would be Adams and Jackson. Gage had a room next to the President's while on the other side and across the hall the rooms were occupied by Gage's men.

Gage and Hunter went over the President's schedule point by point with Gage making notations where to place extra security. It was another hour before Gage was satisfied with the overall itinerary. They were in Gage's room and he fetched them both a glass of whiskey.

Nate lit his eighth cigar of the day and leaned back in the chair. "Now, Jim, fill me in on everything and why you think

142

the President is in any more danger than usual." Hunter took a sip of the whiskey and began with Toby, the grizzly attack, and how Buck Sawtelle had saved his life. He finished his narrative with Lefty's dying words.

Nate did not respond immediately; he was studying the blue smoke rings he was in the habit of making when in deep thought. Hunter got up and helped himself to another whiskey. He was exhausted from the lack of sleep. It seemed a lifetime ago since he had gotten a full night's rest.

"Almighty little to go on, Jim," Gage said, eyeing his tired friend, "but you know how I feel about turning over every rock. And you think the two you're trailing are really after the President?" Hunter nodded. Gage studied the end of his cigar.

"Where's the motive? How much faith can you put in this man, Thompson . . . even on his deathbed. Remember you bested him. Could be his way of getting back at you . . . keep you unsettled."

"Maybe, but I don't think so. As yet I don't have a motive. But you know as well as I do some people don't need one."

Nate looked keenly at Hunter. "So what you aiming to do about it?"

"Find the connection and the two men but not necessarily in that order. I got a personal score to settle with them two as well—for Buck. Figured with the extra men Bounds is providing, you won't need me for a day or two." Nate drained the glass and refilled it for the second and last time while the President was in Denver. He paced the room, puffing on the sweet-smelling cigar.

"All right. But as soon as you get close, you get help."

"I will." Gage waved the cigar in the air.

"If it ultimately protects the President, then I'm satisfied. Besides"—his features softened somewhat—"figure I owe this Buck Sawtelle that much for saving a friend's life." And he raised his glass in a silent salute.

Hunter made his way down the carpeted stairs, feeling the strain of the last few days tugging at his tired body. His eyes felt as if he had ridden through a sandstorm. A few people still lingered in the lobby. The gaslit chandeliers cast a soft, golden glow across the room to highlight the new French brocaded

143

drapes hung just hours before for Grant's party.

He was surprised to find light snow falling as he stepped into the street. A blast of bitter air swept tiny flakes down the street, stinging his eyes and face. The crisp cold cleared his head of alcohol, and in spite of the lateness it gave him a new source of energy. He breathed the tiny flakes deep into his lungs. On impulse he turned down F Street and headed for the Gray Tavern. At this hour there probably wouldn't be much to gain by stopping by, yet he felt compelled to do so.

Hunter stepped into the saloon, pausing to shake the new snow from his coat. The Gray Tavern was like countless others; a few rough-hewn tables and a plank bar resting on empty whiskey barrels. The place had an acrimonious feel about it, and the few rough-clothed patrons contributed heavily to the atmosphere. The stale air was whiskey-laden and smoky. Hunter stepped to the bar. A greasy-looking bartender with wet black eyes glared hard at him.

"What'll it be, mister?" His voice was high-pitched and reminded Hunter of a squeaky wagon wheel. The voice was strange and out of character for someone who stood a good two inches taller than himself.

"Beer." He didn't really want one, but it gave him an excuse for being there. While the barkeep was gone, he studied the diehard crowd. At a table nearest him a gambler type practiced his trade with a desultory hand of solitaire. His broadcloth suit was thin and well worn, reminiscent of better times. Hunter put his age at fifty and heading downhill whiskey-fast by the looks of his puffy face. He turned his attention to the other patrons. They were a mixed lot of grim-faced individuals ranging from hard-rock miners to shifty-eyed weasels with sharp knives at their belts, waiting and watching for the first signs of weakness. He recognized no one. As he turned back to the bar he sensed the gambler giving him the once-over. Professional curiosity? Most likely. Customers were hard to come by at this time of night.

"Ten cents," the bartender said in his strange voice. Hunter laid a double eagle on the counter.

"Keep the change if you can answer a few questions." The big man looked from the gold coin and back again to Hunter.

144

"Depends on what's being asked."

"Fair enough," Hunter replied. He took a sip of the cold beer and noticed in the dingy mirror the gambler had stopped playing cards.

"Understand I might find Lefty Thompson here." The man's face changed sharply to one of caution.

"Don't know no Thompson." His voice was openly hostile now. "Besides, don't figger it's my business to keep up with those a-coming or a-going." The double eagle had disappeared behind the man's dirty apron.

"That case, you owe me change," Hunter said evenly. The bartenders' face flared a deep crimson as he counted out the money. Hunter picked up the money and left the saloon. The gambler had gone back to his cards. Hunter decided to play a hunch. He stationed himself at the corner of the saloon and the alley. In the soft glow of the gas streetlights he could see the snow was getting thick now. A good three inches covered the ground. He didn't have to wait long. Through the swirling white mist he saw the gambler emerge from the saloon and pause on the boardwalk to look down for tracks. Hunter stepped deeper into the shadows as the man headed his way. The gambler knew nothing until he felt the hard prod of a gun at his back and a cold voice from the darkness.

"Stand easy!" Hunter ordered. The gambler stood rooted with his hands at his sides. He swallowed hard, trying to find his voice.

"Jesus . . ." he gulped, "don't shoot. I don't mean you no harm." He felt himself being searched. Hunter found the small derringer in the man's vest pocket. The pressure never let up on the gambler's back.

"Turn down the alley and do it slowly." The gambler did as he was told, keeping his hands in plain view.

"Far enough. What's your name?"

"Ingram. Sam Ingram," he blurted out, the pressure on his spine unrelenting. Ingram was beginning to question his sanity for following the man.

"Well, Mr. Ingram, you out for your nightly constitution . . . or hunting meat?" Ingram heard the unmistakable metallic click of a six-gun going to full cock.

145

"Wait . . . oh, please!" Panic rose hard in Ingram's throat. "I only want to talk . . . honest to God, mister!" A trickle of sweat ran down between his shoulder blades. His mouth had gone dry as desert sand.

"Overheard you ask Squeaky . . . the bartender, about Lefty." Hunter took the gun from Ingram and spun him around.

"Go on," Hunter commanded, seeing the frightened man's eyes in the subdued light.

"Might know this gent if you spare a few dollars."

"Same deal I offered the bartender. Now, talk." Ingram gathered his thoughts now that the gun was no longer prodding his spine.

"I've played a few hands of cards with Lefty from time to time. A sore loser and mean as they come when drinking. Kept this huge knife he stroked like a tomcat." Ingram cleared his throat, wondering if he was doing right. What would keep the man from putting a hole in him once he was done. Ingram started sweating all over again.

"Early last night Lefty dropped by the saloon well-heeled and in a good mood. Things were kinda slow and we played a hand or two. Funny thing, he lost both hands but never complained. He hinted at the chance to make a lot more money once he put a blue-belly to rest." Hunter's heart raced against his rib cage.

"Did he say who he was working for?"

"No. Except what he was going to do would help the South rise from Grant's ashes."

"What!" Hunter shouted. "What about Grant?"

"Hell, mister, everybody that hangs out at the Gray is either an ex-Confederate or a Southern sympathizer. And with Grant due in town, I figgered Lefty was rattling on like most. Only thing is . . . if you're looking for Lefty, you'll have to check O'Neil's ranch," Ingram said, referring to the graveyard named after the gentleman gambler.

"Yes, I know." Ingram was startled.

"But you asked Squeaky . . . ?"

"Here." Hunter placed two double eagles in Ingram's hand. He holstered the Colt and took the two shells from the derringer before handing it back to the dumbfounded gambler.

"You're him, ain't you? The one I read about in the paper?"

"I'm staying at Wootton's Hotel. If you think of anything else, stop by. The name's Hunter." Hunter turned back to the street. Ingram watched as he paused at the mouth of the alley, and suddenly it came to him.

"Mr. Hunter," Ingram called softly. "There was a name Lefty mentioned. Something about settling a personal score with a man named Meeker or Meecham. No, it was Meekam. That was it, Joe Meekam." A bolt of lightning could not have startled Hunter more, and he snapped around to face the darkened alley.

"Did he say where this Meekam was staying?" The snowflakes, bigger now, whispered across the distance separating the two men.

"No, he didn't . . . sorry."

"No matter. I *will* find him. Thanks again, Ingram."

Sam Ingram started to thank the hard-eyed Hunter for the money, but all he saw was blowing snow. Hunter was gone. He was damn glad he wasn't Meekam. He made his living reading men, and Hunter was as tough and dangerous as they come. Ingram rubbed the two cold coins together, creating a warm sensation in the pit of his stomach. He smiled up at the flakes of snow. Tonight, or what was left of it, he would not be sleeping alone.

CHAPTER THIRTY

The spring storm raged all night, adding eight inches to the three already on the ground, while higher up in the foothills and canyons twenty inches of white powder covered the rails. Work crews from the Colorado Central in Black Hawk scurried down the tracks at first light to clear areas where drifts six to eight feet choked both wagon roads and train rails.

Clear Creek, already rabid from spring runoff, began to froth and buck uncontrollably from the additional snow as it tumbled down through steep canyons. Its muddy waters, bloated like a dead steer, became a cauldron of swirling madness as it spewed out of the foothills and raced wildly across the flats tearing into the normally sluggish South Platte with full fury.

By daybreak the storm had abandoned Denver and moved out across the prairie, leaving Cherry Creek inches from overflowing its banks.

Out on the South Platte, men cursed and fought hard against the boiling river as it threatened to rip ferry cables from their moorings. Horses plunged wildly about on the heaving deck, and for a while it looked as though men, horses, and supplies would be sucked into the deadly mass before putting to shore. In the brilliant blue of early morning every sound was sharp and clear in the thin cold air.

Over breakfast of steak and eggs, Hunter told Wootton of his encounter with the gambler and of having tracked the Texan earlier in the day.

"Jasper like that ought not to be too hard to find," Wootton said as he washed the last of his food down with coffee from his big mug.

"What I was thinking. I know Bounds has started searching

the hotels, but it won't hurt if I conduct my own search as well." Hunter pushed back from the table and stood up.

"Want some help?" Wootton asked. "Got nothing better to do except wait fer the next meal." He grinned and patted his ample stomach. Hunter started to protest, but Wootton held up a beefy hand.

"Whether you like it or not, I do know Denver better than you ever will. They's more nooks and crannies to hide more lowlifes than a porkypine has quills."

Hunter stepped out into a sparkling clear day to wait for Wootton to grab his hat and coat. The whiteness hurt his eyes, and he pulled the black felt hat lower on his head. The cold air bit deeply at his lungs. Two blocks south he could hear the cries of men and the sharp snap of bullwhips as the milling mass was being unloaded from the ferry.

Hunter could feel time slipping away, and he was no closer to the men than when he first arrived in Denver. Before they started their search, he would send another wire to army headquarters with Joe Meekam's name. Could be the answer to a lot of questions he was carrying around. He hoped so for President Grant's and Buck's sake.

Meekam rousted Quirt out of bed early and instructed him to pack quickly and meet him downstairs. Bleary-eyed and still punchy from the whiskey, Quirt scrambled around in the alcoholic fog gathering up his things.

Later they slipped into Madame Vestal's office to find the Southern beauty at her desk with several ledgers spread before her.

Her face flushed red upon seeing the pair. "What now?" she demanded. "Thought I made it perfectly clear I want nothing more to do with you."

"Hold on, lady, all we need is a place to lay low for the next couple days. After that we'll be gone." Belle Siddons fought to curb her mounting anger.

"Mr. Meekam, I don't run a boardinghouse." Meekam smiled coldly, ignoring the barb.

"Need a place out of the way but close to town. Figured

you'd know of one."

It took them over an hour of side-street wandering and backtracking before Meekam and Tyler approached the old miner's cabin hidden from general view among brush and giant cottonwoods growing along the Platte. Belle Siddons had purchased the cabin a few years back from a miner who wanted to return to the States. It was located on a site used as a favorite camping ground by the Arapaho and Cheyenne long before the white man probed the area for gold. The Arapahos had shared the lush valley with their neighbors, the Cheyennes, and at times over a thousand Indians were encamped by the normally peaceful Platte. Forgotten and overgrown with weeds, the site still held remnants of the Indians' passings: broken arrowheads, pieces of pottery, and long-cold campfires.

The cabin was remarkably clean and well stocked with basic provisions. Belle told them she used it as a retreat from time to time. It suited Meekam's purposes just fine. Let Hunter track him now, he thought grimly.

Quirt built a fire and had coffee going by the time Tader Snider slipped through the brush and up to the cabin door. He accepted a cup of the hot liquid from Quirt, grateful to be out of the snow and cold. Meekam was scouting their location for escape routes. He didn't intend to be trapped this close to having his plans become a reality.

"Guess we'll find out now what it is we're being so highly paid to do," Tader probed the Texan.

"Guess so," Quirt grunted, skirting the issue. He took his coffee to the cabin's only window and peered out into the cold. Christ, didn't it ever warm up? It looked to him like winter had set in again. A movement in the nearby brush and Quirt caught sight of the fellow Texan, Frank Maxwell.

Later, when everyone was present, Meekam got himself a cup and stood in front of the small, expectant group.

"Anybody having second thoughts?" he asked. His coat was pushed aside, exposing the walnut butt of his six-gun. The hard-bitten men looked at one another, puzzled. Meekam continued. "Hope everyone had a good time because"—here he paused to look at each man—"things gets serious from here on out." A sober atmosphere settled over the room.

"This will be our headquarters until we make our move. We stay here as a group. No one leaves unless I give the okay. Understood?" No one spoke.

"I want two guards posted at all times. One in the front and one in back along the river. There's a possibiity men may be trying to cut our trail, so the less we expose ourselves, the better off we will be." Quirt shifted in his chair, knowing full well Meekam was referring to the Hunter fiasco. He was damned glad he hadn't mentioned Hunter trailing him yesterday.

"Excuse me, Captain," Billy Hamill said in his slow southern drawl, "we aim to stick tight no matter how hard the hound shakes his head. So jest lead on and don't worry none about looking back. Reckon what we all kinda wondering is what you figger on pulling?" The others nodded their heads. Clearly the time had come. Meekam set his cup on the table and lit a cigar.

"As I told you before, what I have planned could advance the Southern cause, although not by much, I admit. But it might help to even the score for those of us who lost relatives and friends to the war." Meekam's eyes turned a smoky gray, and his voice rang out granite hard. But it was Meekam's next words that left each man at the table speechless.

"On Monday we will liberate this country from the hands of the one responsible for spilling so much Southern blood." His face twisted with pure hatred. "We are going to assassinate General Grant!" Meekam refused to call him president.

CHAPTER THIRTY-ONE

It was mid-afternoon before Wootton and Hunter hit pay dirt. The fleabag hotel was in a run-down section of town not two blocks from where he had lost the Texan the day before. The clerk was unshaven and sported a dirty white shirt over which a pair of suspenders, long faded from the original red to a dusty pink, held up a greasy pair of threadbare trousers.

Bitterness welled up inside Hunter when the clerk informed them the pair had left early that morning.

"Could you tell us anything you might know? It is extremely important," Hunter asked the sullen clerk.

"Might know of the two gentlemen but"—he licked dry lips—"something to warm the brain might help my memory."

"I'll give you something to warm yore brain," Wootton said harshly. He jerked the clerk forward in an iron grip by the front of his dirty shirt as if he were nothing more than a piece of paper. Wootton stuck the point of the bowie against the man's bobbing Adam's apple. The clerk shuddered at the feel of cold steel, and his eyes filled with undisguised terror. Less than a heartbeat in time had elapsed.

"Wait a minute, Wootton," Hunter said, following the big man's lead. "Give him a chance to talk, then if he's lying you can slit his gullet."

Luther Jones swallowed dry sand before he could say a word. The man with the knife was wild-looking and he feared for his life like never before.

"Honest to God, mister! Was only hoping fer a little something to wax the throat."

"How 'bout I shellac it with yore blood. Figger you can talk then?" Wootton said, letting the knife point prick the man's skin. The clerk looked close to fainting.

"Here." Hunter tossed a ten-dollar gold piece on the counter. "Now, talk!"

"They were here three days or so, I forget. One was ramrod straight. Kinda hard-faced and quiet. Had eyes looked right through you. The other fellar was a whole lot friendlier and he walked with a roll, like it was his first time off a horse."

"Did you overhear any of their conversations? Did they mention where they were heading from here?"

"They were chicken-lipped tight, but it was plain to see the taller of the two was peeved at the other over something." Hunter wondered about that.

"Don't guess they left a forwarding address?" Wootton asked dryly, releasing the clerk from his grip. He put the big bowie away. Relief flooded Luther's face.

"Quirt was the short one's name. Asked me directions to Ada Lamont's. A real friendly sort."

"Anything else? Like where they ate, habits, or visitors?" Luther scratched his dirty head in thought.

"Come to think of it, couple days ago three tough-looking hombres came in an' went up the stairs without asking fer anybody . . . like they knew where they were going. Looked to me like gunhands." Wootton and Hunter exchanged glances.

"That it?" Hunter asked.

"Wal, funny you mentioned habits. The tall one, called hisself Smith, would sat over to the window and read the paper every morning. But this morning he had barely sat down before he jumped up and ran upstairs. A minute later he was back down again and he paid his bill. Quirt came down shortly and they were gone. All I know." Luther eyed the gold coin, but with the gorilla watching him like a hawk, he dared not pick it up. Hunter's eyes narrowed in thought. What could have been in the paper to cause Meekam to react so? He had not seen the morning paper.

"You got a paper?" Luther reached under the counter and handed Hunter the paper. He quickly scanned the front page. The big news was the arrival of the President and listed his itinerary for the next few days. Nothing there to cause an alarm that Hunter saw. And then he saw it near the bottom of the page and he knew his fears had been correct all along. The caption read:

PRESIDENT GRANT ARRIVES IN DENVER UNDER HEAVY GUARD

The article attempted to tie the near murder of the presidential aide, James Hunter, to yesterday's heavy show of force for the President. It went on to say Marshal Bounds and Sheriff Eaton were conducting an intensive search of all hotels for those suspected of hiring the assassin.

Hunter swore bitterly. Dammit! Why did Bounds say anything to Byers about conducting a search? He slapped the paper down on the counter and stormed out, leaving Wootton and the clerk at a loss.

"What's up, Jim?" Wootton asked as he caught up with Hunter. Hunter stopped in the muddy street that only this morning had been covered with pristine snow.

"Did you know your sheriff is conducting a search too? Bounds tell him?"

"Sounds like Mack Eaton. He'd sell out his mother fer a vote and make sure it made the headlines the next day. Don't blame Bounds, he didn't talk to Byers."

"We came so close." Wootton clapped Hunter on the back.

"Know how you feel, son. No matter who's to blame, we got close enough to smell they tracks. We'll find them again." Hunter looked doubtful. Time was running out. Question was, where did they look next?

In the waning light of late afternoon they recrossed the muddied streets churned to a dirty red consistency by the heavy freight traffic, to Wootton's saloon. Hunter paused on the plank walk to beat some of the stinking mud from his boots. Wootton went on in, paying no mind to the ubiquitous material, as did most of his patrons. Hunter looked at the deeply corduroyed street, its imperfections hidden earlier by last night's snow, and sighed wearily. He wished to be free of this place and its ever-present crowds. Instinctively he looked toward the far mountains and thought of Jay and Buck.

Later he caught up with Nate Gage at the Bellmont House, where Grant was having a private supper with the mayor, John

Routt, and a few selected officials. Hunter had spent the better part of an hour nursing a single drink at a back table at Wootton's, brooding over Meekam and having self-doubts. There was a good chance he was wrong about Meekam. A lot of people made idle threats where the President was concerned. But then, what about the gunmen, and why was Meekam running? What he needed most was a motive to convince Nate as well as himself. The more he thought about it, the more he became convinced the wire to the army could be the pivotal point to this whole affair.

Hunter briefed Gage on the latest news concerning the hurried departure of Meekam and a man called Quirt.

"One thing's for sure," Gage said, keeping a sharp eye on his men and the gathering crowd. "They got something to hide. Question is, what? Buck's shooting or the attempt on your life . . . or both."

Hunter shook his head. "It's more than that. Especially when you bring in three hired guns."

Nate took his eyes from the crowd to look at Hunter keenly.

"So what now? I have to tell you your chances of finding them are pretty low. This is a big place with a lot of places to hide."

A dark gloom settled over Hunter as he headed back to Wootton's. He wished he could hear from the army. The refreezing slush crunched sharply under his boots in the cold air.

CHAPTER THIRTY-TWO

For the better part of the night Hunter slept like someone drugged. Just before the pink rays of early morning touched the higher peaks to the west, the grizzly visited him once more, leaving him drenched and breathing hard. He dressed and went downstairs to find the cook stirring up last night's coals under a pot of coffee.

"Be ready in a jiffy, Mr. Hunter," Willy Simpson said as he rolled up his sleeves to mix a batch of sourdough biscuits.

"No hurry, Shortbread," Hunter said, calling him by the only name he knew. "Need some fresh air anyway."

Hunter stepped through the low-slung back door, wondering idly how many times Wootton had banged his head on the crossbeams.

The cold air of early morning cleared his head and lifted his spirits despite the self-imposed gloom he was under. In the direction of the river he heard the high-pitched scream of a hawk disturbed over something. The sound drew him back to the high country where he belonged, not sitting in some town surrounded by ten thousand people. He sorely missed the Gunnison. No wonder Wootton was leaving.

Hunter slipped the rawhide thong from the new Colt .45 that had been a gift from the President upon his arrival in Denver. With a seven-and-half-inch barrel, the gun had an excellent feel and balance. He palmed the gun with a quick flick of his wrist. The move was fluid and natural, a part of him honed to a fine art requiring no conscious thought on his part.

"Not bad fer a young squirt," Wootton said as he stepped from the outhouse, pulling up his suspenders.

"You lucky I didn't send you some daylight through that door," Hunter said, grinning. He holstered the gun and slipped the thong back in place. Wootton's eyes twinkled as he came up to Hunter.

"One of them new seventy-three Colts, ain't it?" Hunter nodded, embarrassed at having been caught practicing quick draw.

"A gift from the President. Uses metallic cartridges instead of the old paper bullets." Hunter handed Wootton one of the shells.

"Now, ain't that something. Course, I never wuz much with a short gun. Give me my ol' Sharps er a Henry in a real fight and fer close-range conversation ain't nothing like a Greener," Wootton said dryly. The truth was, handgun accuracy was almost always overexaggerated beyond thirty yards. Most stand-up fights occurred at distances of fifteen to twenty paces. A fact Hunter was well aware of.

Over breakfast Wootton told Hunter no one matching Quirt's description had been seen at Ada's place. "Course they's more interested in the color of yore money than yore physical attributes."

"Figured that for a dead end anyway." Bounds came through the door with a paper in his hand. Hunter's temper flared for a moment.

"Drag up a chair, Frank, I'll have Shortbread fix you some breakfast," Wootton said. Bounds hesitated, looking from Wootton to Hunter.

"Sit down, Marshal," Hunter said, tight-lipped. Bounds took a seat.

"For the record, it wasn't me told Byers we were searching the hotels. I talked to Sheriff Eaton. Guess he went straight to Byers. Sorry you missed Meekam. Wootton told me about it last night."

"Forget it. What's done is done. You got something for me?"

Bounds tossed the wire to Hunter. "From Marshal Townsend in Santa Fe." Shortbread brought Bounds a plate of food and more coffee for everyone.

"I knew it!" Hunter banged his fist on the table.

"Knew what?" Wootton asked, mopping his plate clean with a biscuit.

Hunter smiled broadly. "Meekam was released from prison only three weeks ago. Served nine of a fifteen-year sentence for armed robbery. His accomplice is still at large."

"Explains why he never came back fer the Reynolds gold afore now," Wootton said. "Guess you were right about Meekam all along, Jim."

"Now, if I could just hear from army headquarters," Hunter said.

"I been meanin' to tell you," Wootton said. "Remember the other day when you wuz askin' Frank about finding the Reynolds gang dead. Wal, I recollect something Colonel Chivington, the same gent responsible for the disgraceful carnage at Sand Creek, said to me. You see, I wuz the one found them pilgrams a-standing upright tied to trees. Shot and stripped 'cept fer the boots they stood in. Kinda hard fer a man tied to a tree to escape, but that was Chivington's story . . . at least till I come up on them fellars with their flesh a-falling off. Later during one of Chivington's drinking bouts he admitted to me he shot Jim Reynolds himself. Said just before he shot him, Reynolds told him as long as two still rode the trail, the gang would never die." Hunter's eyes blazed with excitement.

"Then Meekam must be one of the gang."

"Looks that way, don't it." Hunter wondered if Quirt was the other gang member . . . or was it the one he left lying in the canyon.

"The way I read it too," Bounds said between sips of hot coffee.

"Course, that still don't mean he's gunning fer the President."

"Maybe, but I bet my new Colt he is."

Later Hunter descended the stairs, looking clear-eyed and fit. He had shaved and changed to a dark suit. The new Colt rested comfortably on his hip. The grizzly incident was at once safely locked away. He met Jenkins at the bottom of the stairs red-eyed and disheveled.

"Just coming up to bring you this wire," Jenkins said in a tired voice. Hunter took the wire, promising Jenkins his help would not be forgotten. Jenkins left, wishing someone would tell that to his wife. He had spent so much time at the office, she had accused him of seeing another woman.

Hunter tore open the wire from the army, feeling his heart pounding in his chest. Finally it was here. What he needed to prove Meekam's intentions. He had to find Nate. The President was in real danger. Hunter pulled on his heavy coat and stepped into the clear cold, yet to the west over the high peaks a dark storm was gathering.

The thought struck him squarely as he headed off to find Nate. If not for the grizzly attack, none of the rest would have happened and Meekam's chances of success would be better than even. He shivered inwardly at the thought.

Hunter caught up with Nate and the President at a fund-raising luncheon sponsored by John Routt. Their goal was to sway President Grant to their cause for statehood.

The territorial governor was speaking when Hunter entered the room.

". . . The Colorado Territory is ripe for statehood, and we offer 'the States' untold sources of new wealth in view of today's economic gloom. In addition, Mr. President, we promise to provide you with solid political backing for your position with Congress. The rest of the country needs our natural resources and land to build a future on if this great country of ours is to continue spreading westward." What Routt didn't know and Hunter did was that the President had been sold on the idea of statehood for Colorado a long time before.

It was after Otto Mears and Chief Ouray had departed from Washington that Grant had learned of Hunter's desire to move to Colorado. Grant had encouraged him to settle on the Gunnison, saying statehood was not too far in the future. Hunter had been surprised at how much Grant knew about the territory, and now, as he listened to him speak, Grant put this knowledge to good use.

As he finished speaking, the people roared their approval and surged around the one person who could lead them to statehood. All semblance of security dissolved in the enthusiastic onslaught. Nate Gage looked like a sick cow with a bellyfull of locoweed.

Hunter nodded to Bounds as he watched the crowd from his

side of the room. The President was completely hidden from view by the crush of people.

"Looks like the President's having a good time," Hunter said quietly as he sidled up to Nate. Gage looked around at Hunter.

"You're back on the job," he growled. "Get to watching this crowd. You know what to do."

"That's why I'm here," Hunter said with a smile. "Looks like the only way to smoke Meekam out into the open is with the President." Gage turned a sickly green, and he took his eyes off the milling crowd for a moment to study Hunter.

"You look like a catbird that's caught a two-foot worm." Hunter smiled broadly, the scar tingling his face.

"Yeah, and I got the worm right here," he said, patting his coat pocket.

"Glad to hear it, but right now let's ease the President out before we live to regret it," Nate whispered softly.

The small knot of men in the cabin by the Platte spent Sunday in thoughtful silence. Each man handled the news of what they were about to do in his own way and time. The magnitude of it sunk in slowly, yet Meekam saw none of their tough resolve weakening. Even Quirt, who had taken over the cooking chores, remained steadfast.

As darkness gathered outside, and while they were eating, Meekam carefully laid out his plan for the next morning. Few questions were asked; none were needed outside of timing and the responsibility of each man. The plan was simple and required little preparation. Meekam had learned long before, while riding with Reynolds, the simpler a plan was, the greater the chances for success. And Meekam intended to have the plan succeed. It had to. He had lived for nothing else for so long.

As the men turned back to their meal in silence, distant thunder spoke of another approaching spring storm.

CHAPTER THIRTY-THREE

Tired from the day's activities, President Grant lay across his bed staring up at the ceiling with the butt of a cold cigar clamped in his teeth. Across the room Gage and Hunter sat discussing the latest wire from army headquarters.

"Damn Benton's black hide," Nate said quietly. "Somehow I always knew he would come back to haunt the President one day. Too high-handed for my taste."

"Meekam won't back off. He probably planned something like this ever since that day. He'll use whatever means he can to get to the President."

"Explains the hired guns," Nate said grimly. "Any ideas on when and where they will hit us?"

"Got a feeling they'll wait till we got our defenses strung out. Train maybe, or the open trail."

"Not in the city?" Nate questioned.

"Less chance for success. And Meekam is driven to see that it succeeds."

"The train, huh. Tomorrow?"

"My best guess. They could wait and hit us on the road to Central City or Georgetown. Dunno. Hard to say. What we need is to do the unexpected. Something Meekam is not likely to know about or suspect," Hunter said, looking over at the still form on the bed.

"You mean the trick we pulled with the major when Lincoln was top dog?"

"It worked," Hunter said simply. Gage had to admit it worked like a charm. He and Hunter both worked for Major E. J. Allen, one of the many aliases Allan Pinkerton used, helping him establish the country's first secret service as directed by President Lincoln. It was during one of Lincoln's trips Gage

161

and Hunter had prevented his assassination by putting the President on an earlier train from Baltimore to Washington.

"He's not going to like it," Nate said.

"You talk to him, Nate."

"Correction, *we* talk to him."

"Talk to me about what?" Grant asked from the bed. Nate's expression was pained.

"Forgot he has ears like a turkey," Gage said loudly to Hunter. "Did I tell you of the time General Grant stood on one side of the Rapidan and listened to what the Confederates was planning for the next day's battle? Hadn't been for his keen hearing, we would have lost the fight." Hunter smiled in spite of the seriousness of the situation. But Nate was like that. The more tense things got, the more relaxed he became. Only when idle did Gage become ill tempered.

Grant sat up on the bed and studied his two aides, an amused look touching his quiet eyes. The two men pulled their chairs closer to the bed.

"Jim just received proof an attempt will be made on your life tomorrow . . . or within the next day or two." Grant said nothing, his calm features as stoic as ever over the bad news.

"Mr. President, what Nate is saying is I got a wire from army headquarters. One of the men I've been tracking, Joe Meekam, deserted the Union Army at Shiloh along with his younger brother, Billy Meekam. Story has it, Billy shot it out with Benton's troops after they caught him stripping a field pack from a dead Federal soldier. His brother evaded capture. Now, in addition to this, I have circumstantial proof this Joe Meekam rode with the Reynolds gang here in Colorado. They were supposed to steal gold for the South, but I think all they took went into their own pockets." It was a few minutes before Grant said anything, quietly chewing on the dead cigar.

"Looks like Captain Benton is reaching out from the grave. You two ought to be satisfied"—Grant smiled—"since neither of you thought much about his tactics." Hunter recalled the only time he had met the swaggering Jack Benton, an individual who held life so contemptuously cheap . . . especially a soldier's.

Their meeting occurred late one night following a long and

hard-fought battle begun before daybreak and lasting well into the night. Everyone was exhausted and casualties were especially heavy on the Union side. Benton came into camp during a heavy thunderstorm. He was with Grant at the time and the swarthy-faced man stepped into Grant's tent flinging water everywhere. He neither saluted nor apologized for his entrance and the showering he gave General Grant. Benton's uniform was grimy and mud-splattered and he reeked of sweat and cheap whiskey.

"General Grant, my men have taken over forty deserters in the last twenty-four hours and with your permission we will begin execution at dawn." Grant, himself weary from the prolonged battle in hostile weather, lit a cigar and studied the rain-soaked officer who slouched before him. Lightning streaked the black night, casting their shadowy figures on the side of the tent for a second. Morale was at a low point. The men had been fighting hard without much rest, unmindful of the mud and drenching rains for over four days now. What they needed was a day to get their bodies and spirits together again, warm clothes, dry beds, and hot food. Grant had no doubt the Confederates were in the same shape.

"Captain Benton, you will see those men returned to their respective units." Benton's face registered deep surprise, and anger rose in his throat.

"But, sir, these men are deserters. They—"

"They are like you and me, Benton," Grant said, cutting off his outburst, "tired of the fighting and killing, and wondering when it will ever end." Benton snapped his mouth shut, brought himself to full attention, anger running in him deep. He stepped back into the storm without another word.

"Didn't do that out of some sudden charity or because you were present. As much as you dislike the man, he does serve a useful function." And that was all he ever said on the subject between them.

And now, as Hunter pieced together his findings for President Grant, he realized just how much events from the past were shaping future actions.

"Meekam holds you personally responsible for his brother's death," Hunter said.

Grant, not one to shirk responsibility, replied, "As he should. Benton was operating under my direct orders."

"That may be, Mr. President," Gage interjected, "but a lot of others were shot as deserters, too, yet you don't see their relatives out gunning for you."

"This man obviously cared a great deal for his brother." Grant puffed on the dead cigar out of habit.

"Or Benton made a grave mistake and this Billy Meekam was no deserter at all. Regardless, Meekam, I feel, has every intention of seeing you dead."

"The way I read it too, Mr. President," Gage added soberly.

"Accepted. What are you proposing?" Here it comes, Hunter thought. This is where they earn their money. Convincing Grant to take evasive measures would not be easy. Two things he didn't care for—one was backtracking and the other concern for his personal safety.

Nate Gage cleared his throat. "Jim and I think Meekam will try to hit you while you are on the train."

"Train?" Grant responded. "You two thinking of pulling that same trick with me as you did with Abe?"

"You must admit it did work," Gage said with satisfaction. The President frowned deeply.

"Mr. President," Hunter added, "before you say no, would you at least consider it as a favor to me. If Buck Sawtelle had not troubled himself over me after the grizzly attack, I wouldn't be here now and we wouldn't know of Meekam's plans either. With you on an earlier train, we can concentrate on Meekam if he decides to make his move."

Nate picked up the defense. "Once we get to Black Hawk, we can slip you aboard the presidential car and nobody will be the wiser."

Grant looked at Hunter with steady eyes. "I'll do it for you and your friend if it allows you the chance to catch the perpetrators, not out of fear for my life."

"Thank you, Mr. President," Hunter said with obvious relief.

"We will attend to the details tonight," Gage said. They left the President under heavy guard. Henry Teller didn't know it yet, but he was in for a long night.

CHAPTER THIRTY-FOUR

At first light, under threatening, low skies, Hunter left Wootton nursing his big coffee cup and returned to the hotel where the President was staying. It was up to him now to see Meekam paid for his deeds. He only hoped what they were doing would bring Meekam out; otherwise, they were going to be in for a rough time trying to cover every rock and hill on the trail. Through Benton's act so long ago, the President of the United States was now in grave danger. Nothing could be done about the past, but he sure as hell intended to do something about the present. A light snow began to fall as he increased his determined stride.

Henry Teller met Hunter in the lobby, looking tired and disheveled.

"Everything is ready. Took most of the night, but the work train is here now and we can get under way as soon as the President is ready."

"We appreciate your cooperation in this matter, Mr. Teller," Hunter said warmly. "I trust few people know of this?"

"Not even those operating the train, sir, but I must tell you that on such short notice I can offer few amenities on a crew train."

"The President understands the necessity for such measures. No need to apologize."

"I rented the carriage you asked for."

"Fine. I'll drive everyone over myself."

Later, Hunter and Henry Teller watched from the station platform as Grant and Nate Gage boarded the work train. No one else was around at this hour. The wet snowflakes cast a bleak picture across the cold landscape, but patches of blue could be seen through the broken cloud layer over the distant mountains. It promised to be a beautiful day where they were heading.

"Sure you don't want me to stay and you go in my place?" Gage asked Hunter.

"We've been through that already," Hunter replied with a warm smile that pulled the scar on his jaw fiddle-string tight. "See you in Black Hawk in a few hours."

Nate's face sobered. "Take care, Jim." He closed the door behind him to the sleeping quarters usually reserved for the rail crews. The unscheduled train gave two sharp blasts from the steam whistle and slowly pulled away from the station. Behind it sat the spit-shined presidential train waiting for the special guest who would never show.

Hunter and Teller stood together in the slackening snowfall, silently watching the short train grow smaller. Hunter felt immense relief by having the President out of town and safe for the moment.

"Best get back to the hotel, Mr. Teller, and make ready for the President's grand departure from this fair city," Hunter said dryly.

South of town, Tader Snider and Billy Hamill crossed the South Platte, leading three newly purchased saddle horses. An early cold mist hung over the Platte despite the thinning snow. The mist clung to them momentarily as they cleared the other side of the riverbed and pointed their horses toward the far mountains. In the distance they heard the sharp blast of the Colorado Central work train as it cleared the station.

They had been Sam Tappen's first customers, buying two sticks of dynamite and a box of .44 cartridges. Dressed now in plain riding garb, Snider and Hamill looked nothing like hopeful prospectors to Tappen, especially with such a scant supply list. The thought disturbed him vaguely, but once they were gone, he returned to sweeping the boardwalk free of the litter of the night before, the two men forgotten.

Tader worked a boulder-size lump of tobacco to his left cheek and emptied his mouth of the brown liquid.

"You think his plan will work?" he asked his riding companion. Billy shifted his gaze from the snow-crested mountains to Tader's frank face.

"Dunno, Tader," he said solemnly. "I do know this much—if we pull it off, we'll be the most hated and hunted men in the history of this country." The sobering thought left both men silent as they continued to ride toward the rugged mountains. The die had been cast, and for these hard men, to do otherwise never crossed their minds.

Meekam, Frank Maxwell, and Quirt Tyler left the cabin dressed in dark broadcloth suits and caught the horse-drawn streetcar to Union Depot. It wouldn't do to show up with muddied clothes and shoes when they were supposed to be big-city reporters. They found the station platform filled with a high-spirited crowd and it was easy for them to mingle without notice. They worked their way into a group of newsmen and reporters waiting to board the narrow-gauge train. The mist from their combined breathing hung over the group of men like a low cloud in the cold air.

Meekam knew there was some risk in what they were doing, yet with the ever-swelling crowd, identification would be difficult at best . . . and only one man knew their identities.

A clean-shaven fellow next to Meekam introduced himself as Patty McKorkle and asked what newspaper Meekam worked for.

"The *Santa Fe Examiner*, and yourself?" Meekam asked with feigned interest. He took two cigars from a breast pocket and offered one to McKorkle, who swayed against him, and Meekam could smell whiskey on the man's breath.

"*St. Louis Chronicle*," McKorkle replied, puffing slightly on the newly lit cigar. "How's the weather down your way?"

"Almighty cold," Meekam answered, his mind flashing back to the bare prison cell he knew so well. Billy smiled at him from the thicket near the river, and for a second the smell of blood and gunpowder was strong in his nostrils.

"Understand we are to be served a fine breakfast this morning?" he probed McKorkle. Wouldn't do now to have his plans changed at this late date.

"To be sure, Mr. . . . ?"

"Tom Bateman," Meekam replied, recalling the name from a by-line in the *Examiner*, his only luxury while in prison.

"Ah, yes, Mr. Bateman, as I started to say, we are to feast on such delicacies as Rocky Mountain trout, breast of quail sautéed in its own golden juices, and other tidbits too delicious to mention." Evidently Meekam had struck a cord in Patty McKorkle. His love of food was as great, it seemed, as his love of alcohol. While McKorkle talked, Meekam probed the crowds with hawklike eyes. Strange, but he hadn't spotted a single lawman. Off to his left, Quirt and Frank Maxwell conversed in low tones.

McKorkle pulled a flask from an inside pocket. "Care for a touch of the heather to ward off the ague, Mr. Bateman?" McKorkle's eyes were bloodshot, and it was obvious he was well on his way to being drunk, yet his charm and wit were still intact and functional. Meekam declined the offer. McKorkle helped himself to a generous portion of the whiskey. For a moment he closed his eyes, savoring the taste of the potent liquid.

"Ah, Tommy boy, I can almost smell the moors," McKorkle said, lapsing into his Irish brogue.

"Shall we board, sir?" Meekam asked as people around them began to get on the train. Meekam nudged the flushed reporter in the right direction. He wanted seats nearest the dining car. There was no worry since most journalists and VIPs tended to gather in those seats near the rear of the car to be as close to the President as they could. As if this offered some advantage over those who took seats farther away.

Meekam and McKorkle took seats on the front row while Quirt and Maxwell sat directly behind them.

Twenty minutes later the gleaming train cleared the station and Meekam felt a strange tingling sensation to think Grant was only a few short yards away.

Beside him McKorkle rattled on about the West, the newspaper business, and anything else that suited the fancy of the loose-tongued Irishman. Outside of an occasional grunt or nod, Meekam ignored the drunken man.

Quirt rubbed his sweaty palms on his pants while listening to the pounding of his heart in his ears like the steady clicks of the steel wheels over the rails. In less than an hour all hell would break loose and he was clearly unsure of whether he would survive past that point. Why hadn't he just ridden away as he started to do several times? Why had he let it go this far? He sure as hell wasn't doing it for the South . . . or for Toby. Money. Enough money to be somebody back in Texas. Without it he was nothing more than a two-bit cowhand. What he had to do was keep his wits about him if he intended to survive this. Dead men didn't need money.

McKorkle fell into a fitful drunken stupor, the empty flask still clutched in his hand. Meekam was relieved. He checked his watch. Thirty minutes to go. He snapped the lid shut, completely at ease with himself. In a little while he would likely die, but so would his most hated enemy.

CHAPTER THIRTY-FIVE

Hunter sat quietly in Henry Teller's private car reserved for President Grant. He thought of Jay and wondered if Buck would still be alive once he was through here. Henry Teller sat with Sidney Dillon from the Union Pacific discussing railroad business while Al Jackson sat smoking a cigar and listening to their conversation. Hunter admitted that even a short distance away and with his hat on, Al Jackson could easily pass for Grant.

The tension was strong in Hunter, and he got up to pace back and forth across the rich, thick carpet. Much like the Union Pacific's car outfitted for Grant's trip west, Teller's car was every bit as richly decorated down to the well-stocked liquor cabinet and overstuffed leather chairs. His pacing took him to the front of the car, and he opened the door to speak with one of his men.

"How is everything, Tolin?" The lanky special agent was their last line of defense, and he wanted to make sure he remained alert. Hunter liked the younger man, who was a crack shot with a Winchester. His collar was turned up against the raw, cold wind, but his blue eyes sparkled with life.

"Howdy, Jim. Everything's fine so far."

"Keep your eyes peeled. Got a strong hunch things will heat up plenty before long."

"Don't worry," he said, holding the Winchester up, "we can do some heating too." His reddened nose dripped steadily in the rushing wind.

"Why don't you go up front and grab yourself a cup of coffee. I'll stand guard for a few minutes. I could use the air." With a big grin, Tolin handed Hunter the carbine.

"Let me warn you, you'll get all the fresh air you can stand.

Won't be long." He stepped into the next car which was loaded with news reporters.

Hunter took a deep lungful of the arctic air and looked at the bleak high canyon walls of rock on either side of the gently rocking train. He realized just how helpless he was in preventing an attack from any point along these rugged mountains. Thank God the President was with Nate.

Tolin stepped into the crowded car of newsmen. The draft created by the open door sent a shaft of cold air rushing down the aisle like a frozen branding iron on bare flesh and brought howls of protest from several easterners.

Meekam turned casually in his seat to look at the intruder, noting the long coat and wind-reddened face. Whoever he was, he wasn't riding inside. Meekam turned to face the front. Tolin passed without looking right or left, bent on getting something hot to drink at the same time thinking of Hunter on the cold platform.

One of Grant's guard dogs, Meekam thought. Question was, where did they keep this one chained? The platform, most likely, next to Grant's door. He couldn't see putting a man on top of the train in this weather, but one never knew. It was something to keep in mind.

A few minutes later the guard hurried back through the car once more and out the rear. Meekam wondered if there was more than one guard back there in the cold. No matter, in fifteen minutes he would know for sure. What he worried about most was running into Hunter before he had a chance to get to Grant. And the simple plan he had devised offered the greatest element of surprise . . . at least for a few precious seconds.

Meekam felt the sudden change in forward motion coupled with the labored pounding of the train's engine. It told him they had reached the first of two steep grades that would mark the beginning—and for him the end. At the onset of the second grade he would set his plan in motion. He checked his watch and consulted the notations in his notebook. Only two minutes late. Close enough. Beside him McKorkle snored loudly, unaware of what the next few minutes would bring. Tader and Billy Hamill waited at the top of the second steep grade.

Meekam stood up, feeling his muscles tighten. Every movement and every sound seemed to be magnified to him. No one took notice of him or the two men who followed him onto the car's platform. The cutting edge of the cold wind between the space separating the two cars was like an icy tonic to them. Meekam climbed to the top of the car and checked both directions. There were no guards riding on top, at least none he could see. He dropped back to the platform. The self-doubt was plain to see on Quirt's face.

"Let's move," Meekam ordered, and he crossed over to the dining car and opened the door. The car was resplendent in white linen, cut crystal, and flowers on every table. They moved rapidly down the aisle to where a black steward was arranging silverware. He looked up at the determined men as they approached.

"Gentlemen, it will be a few mo' minutes befo' the dining car is open." Meekam drew his gun from beneath his coat and stuck it in the man's belly.

"You so much as breathe heavy and I'll blow your bread basket loose for you." The steward's eyes seemed to grow right out of his head. All he could do was nod his head.

"Move it," Meekam ordered, prodding him with his gun. The steward complied with Meekam's order, backing all the way to the end of the dining car with the gun buried in his ample stomach. Meekam stopped him at the door.

"How many back there?" he demanded.

"Uh . . . they's only three others, suh. Two of dem is cooks and one mo' like me."

"No guards?" Meekam asked sharply.

"No, suh." The black man's voice shook uncontrollably.

"Turn around and move careful like. If you're lying, just remember, I'll fill your stomach with pieces of your backbone." The steward was sweating profusely, and he turned slowly, like an arthritic old man. The cold steel pressed hard against his spine, and it was all he could do to keep from falling down.

A few moments later the trio had the two cooks and the other steward backed against the cook stoves. A large silver tray was being loaded with food when they entered the cook car.

Meekam looked the men over carefully. The second steward was sullen-faced and showed no signs of fear. The two cooks looked on with interest, but an underlying fear for their lives was evident.

"You"—Meekam pointed his gun at a burly cook—"shuck that jacket and hat." The cook hesitated for a moment.

"I said now!" Meekam brought the gun to full cock. The cook needed no further urging. Meekam felt the floor of the car level off again and he made a mental note of it. They had reached the short flat section of track separating the two steep grades. Everything was going as planned.

Meekam motioned for Maxwell to don the white jacket and hat. The fit was nearly perfect. The only other man in the room close to Meekam's size was the angry black steward, and he winced mentally at the thought of wearing his clothes.

"Outa the jacket, blackie," Meekam ordered. This was no time to worry about color. Quirt and Maxwell covered the men while Meekam slipped the black's outfit on. The hat was a little big, but he would manage. Quirt thought they both looked silly and he was glad he had not been asked to wear one.

"This the tray being prepared for the . . . for Grant?" Meekam still could not bring himself to call him by his official designation.

"Don't tell them nuthin'," the sullen steward said. Meekam looked at the belligerent black man and back again to the two cooks, who lowered their eyes under his stare.

"Shoot the nigger if he says another word."

"My pleasure," Quirt said, and pointed his gun at the man's chest. He was feeling there was a strong possibility he might come through this alive. If he could just make it to the horses . . . hope bolstered his courage to a new high.

Meekam felt the locomotive go into labor a second time. It was time.

"Cover the tray," he said to one of the cooks, "and hand me the coffeepot," he told the other.

"Pick up the tray, Frank." Maxwell had trouble keeping the big tray level and it took both hands to steady it.

"You gonna have to open the door for me," Maxwell called over his shoulder, not daring to take his eyes from the

173

quivering tray. His arms were as stiff as frozen aspen limbs in winter.

"Tyler, they're yours. Just do your job, man. All I ask."

Quirt shifted his gaze to Meekam for a second. He had drawn the easiest job and he knew it.

"Luck, Joe," he said softly. "I mean it." Meekam nodded to his cousin and opened the door for Maxwell. A short walk away and he would change history. He heard Billy call to him on the wind as they gained the platform.

"Walk as fast as you can through the news car and keep the tray held high so as to block your face. They will be expecting two stewards, so we shouldn't have any trouble."

Maxwell didn't bother telling Meekam that what they were expecting were two *black* stewards. But hell, it really didn't matter, not now. For in his own way he was much like Meekam, but he suspected for different reasons, still too painful to think about without bringing back all the anger and hurt. He had returned to Texas after the war only to learn his homestead had been burned by a bunch of drunken Yankee soldiers claiming rebels were hiding inside. People said the woman's screams could be heard over the roaring fire and gunshots. The soldiers only laughed and continued to fire into the burning building. Along with his wife he had lost a baby he had never seen. And for that one reason he was more than willing to give his life to see Grant fall.

The cold air rushed inward and momentarily revived McKorkle from his stupor. He tried to focus his bleary eyes on Meekam.

"Don't I know you, sir?" he mumbled thickly. They brushed past McKorkle before he could go farther.

Someone shouted as they passed by. "When do we get to eat?" Others joined in. When they got to the end of the car, Meekam called back.

"Cook said to file into the dining car. Serving will begin in five minutes."

The crowded car came to life all at once as the journalists jostled their way toward the front. Meekam wanted as many people as possible away from the presidential car. He wanted no trouble from that quarter. Meekam checked his gun under the white smock and readjusted it slightly.

"Ready?" he asked Maxwell softly. Frank Maxwell nodded, and taking a deep breath, Meekam opened the door.

Tader cocked his ear to catch the faint sound on the whistling wind charging down the draw from the Continental Divide, a cold as if it had come off a polar ice cap.

They were huddled in a small draw among a few scattered boulders and scraggly wind-bent spruce and alpine fir fighting hard to maintain their lofty perch in the thin, rocky soil. Their horses, their tails turned to the wind, were tied to a stunted aspen nearby.

"That's it, Billy," Tader said, standing up. Billy Hamill was crouching on the leeward side of a large rock, sunning himself. Instantly he was on his feet, stomping around to get some feeling into them. At this elevation the snow was still two or three feet deep. Hamill retrieved the two sticks of explosives from his saddlebags. He paused to light a cigar with steady hands.

"Let's ease down to those rocks near the tracks," Hamill said, watching as the wind whipped the thread of blue smoke from his cigar across the rocky landscape. "That way we can swing aboard at the last minute without anyone seeing us."

A half mile away the train began its laborious ascent up the last steep grade leading into Black Hawk. The engineer, Lucky Curtis, pushed the throttle forward to the wall, listening to the steady thump of the old engine against the red-hot firebox. Lucky had been with Henry Teller since the beginning, and he had experienced everything the mountains could throw at him in one fashion or other. No two rides up these treacherous grades were ever the same in winter. Avalanches, blinding snowstorms that wiped away the rails just ten feet in front of you, and slippery tracks coated heavily with ice were the most unnerving of the daily challenges. Yet Lucky Curtis, as did most train engineers, loved his job and the freedom it provided.

He spit a stream of brown liquid out the side window and called to his tallow pot. "Keep a-feedin' her, Jonesy. She'll eat wood now like it was sweetcake to git over this last hump."

Jonesy's young body glistened with sweat in the red glow of the firebox as he picked up his pace. This was his first time out as a road fireman. He had worked his way up from wiper to engine watchman in less than a year and was switch-engine fireman when he got the call to ride No. 457 with Lucky Curtis with none other than the President of the United States on board. That was really something, he thought as he shoved more wood into the firebox.

At best, Lucky figured they would be doing between eight and ten miles per hour when they hit the top of the grade, what with the strong head wind roaring down at them from the Divide. The best he had ever done was thirteen. No matter, she'd come flying off this summit like a gut-shot antelope. He'd give the President a little ride down the other side, he figured. Yessiree. He shot another load of tobacco juice into the cold wind and turned his attentions to his gauges.

CHAPTER THIRTY-SIX

"Sit down, James. You've been prancing up and down like a stallion in heat for the last half hour," Al Jackson said good-naturedly. "That is an order from your new President."

Hunter stopped his striding long enough to look at his bearded friend. They went back a long way together.

"Sorry, boss. Guess I'm just a little spooked Meekam hasn't made a move," he said, carrying the ruse a bit further.

"No need to be," Jackson said as he lit another cigar. He had the tip glowing red before he continued. "What's the worse can happen? I get shot maybe, but the President is still safe. And you get to capture the bad—"

"What was that!" Hunter interrupted. Instinctively he had drawn his gun and faced the door.

"Didn't hear anything. Relax, will you," Jackson said. "You gonna give me indigestion before I even eat. By the way, didn't you say Tolin said breakfast was coming in five minutes? Been the longest five minutes for a starving man." Hunter holstered his gun and wandered aimlessly toward the rear of the parlor car for lack of something better to do. Could he have been wrong in judging Meekam's intentions?

Tolin crossed over to the news car to avoid as much of the direct wind as he could. Stood to reason he could guard the presidential car from a few feet away as well as keep his exposed flesh from freezing. Frankly he doubted there would be an attempt made at all. Besides, it wasn't as if they were really guarding the President anyway.

The train's speed dropped steadily as it approached the crest some fifty yards distant.

Tolin felt the news car open behind him, and he half turned to see a silver tray covered with a white cloth being carried high by a white-jacketed steward. He had both hands in his pockets while the Winchester was held lazily in the crook of one arm.

"'Bout time. You got a hungry bunch of fellows over there." Maxwell only grunted. From behind, Meekam spoke, half hidden by the door and Maxwell.

"Catch that door for us."

"Sure thing," Tolin said, turning to cross to the other door. Instantly Meekam stepped around Maxwell and laid the barrel of his gun alongside Tolin's skull. The security agent dropped without a whimper. Meekam failed to catch the rifle, and it rattled loudly as it hit the metal platform and bounced over the side.

Both men froze, expecting the other door to swing open any second. Meekam was coiled as tight as a new leather lariat. Nothing happened. He motioned Maxwell to the presidential door.

"Just remember, Grant is mine," he whispered, "you take out whoever else is in the way." Maxwell nodded, shifting the tray to one hand as a real steward would. He turned the door-knob slowly until it opened and then reached under the white jacket for his gun.

Henry Teller was the first one to catch sight of the silver tray.

"Ah, gentlemen, I believe breakfast has arrived." His broad grin quickly faded as he saw the man behind the tray with the cold eyes.

How long had they been gone? Quirt thought. Five minutes? Ten? Hell, every second seemed like an hour. He had backed all four men to the rear of the kitchen in preparation for his leaving. The sullen-faced black cook studied his every move as if waiting his chance. In truth, he was. Since being herded near the door, his coat, where he kept an old pistol, was within arm's reach. The others seemed content to stand by.

Quirt cracked the door and peered out quickly while keeping his gun trained on the men. The platform was empty. He snapped his head back around. No one had moved.

"Won't be but another minute and I'll be gone with nobody hurt long as you do what I say," Quirt said to the watchful men. The black man never took his eyes off Quirt. The train was slowing down even more, and Quirt figured he'd leave about the same time Tader and Billy jumped the engine. No need for him to get caught up in the fracas sure to come.

He opened the door all the way and looked at the rocky walls sliding by slowly. They were close to the summit as near as he could figure. Quirt turned back to see the steward pulling back the hammer on an old percussion pistol. He froze for an instant as the 'fifty-eight Remington spit fire at him. The big bullet caught Quirt in the side and slammed him backward into the doorjamb. His face was one of disbelief that quickly faded to pain. It couldn't be happening . . . all he wanted was to get away. The other men scattered, looking for a place to hide. Quirt thumbed back the hammer on his Colt as he brought the gun to bear on the black man. Their shots went off simultaneously. The kitchen was filled with black smoke as the bullets ripped into each man's flesh. The second slug sent Quirt staggering through the door and onto the platform. He sat down hard, watching the blood spreading fast from the hole in his midsection. Quirt's shot winged the steward, and he dropped the heavy Remington. Calmly he bent down to retrieve the weapon with his good hand and walked over to where Quirt was rapidly going into shock. Breathing heavily, Quirt stared up at the impassive black face. A perplexed look crossed his face. It wasn't supposed to happen this way.

"Why?" he managed to ask weakly. The steward bent down to take his gun.

"Because de President fought to free us coloreds. Only right I should help him." Quirt grimaced in pain. He coughed hard and rolled onto his side. In a minute he got his breath back.

"All your kind thinks next to Lincoln, Grant's the Second Coming."

"Some folks just nebber know when to let things be," the steward answered solemnly.

By the time Hunter realized what was happening, Meekam

and Maxwell were two steps into the parlor car. By then it was too late. Meekam leapt from behind Maxwell, his gun on full cock. He spied Grant sitting in a large overstuffed chair, smoking a cigar.

"Grant! Damn your black soul, this is for Billy!" Meekam screamed. He fired two shots that caught Jackson squarely in the chest. Hunter drew the new Colt before Meekam had finished speaking and fired at Maxwell, who dropped the large tray and returned Hunter's fire. His only shot grooved the mahogany panel above Hunter's head as Maxwell felt the heavy slugs tear into his heart. He was dead before he hit the floor. Meekam, seeing Maxwell go down, snapped a quick shot at Hunter and stepped to one side in the smoke-filled car for one last shot at Grant. Jackson took the third slug two inches from the other wounds. Sure Grant was done for, Meekam leapt back through the doorway as Hunter fired one last time. Hunter swore savagely under his breath and started for the door as he heard gunfire in the distance. Suddenly a tremendous explosion rocked the whole train and all forward motion ceased. The shock threw Hunter to the floor.

CHAPTER THIRTY-SEVEN

Tader and Billy Hamill boarded the locomotive easily, taking the engineer and fireman by surprise. Lucky Curtis opened his mouth to speak, but Tader cut him off.

"Say one word and it will be your last." Tader prodded the engineer with his gun. "Ease up on that throttle." Lucky did as he was told. Meanwhile, Billy covered the fireman while he held the two sticks of explosives in the other. The stub of his cigar glowed red. Lucky looked over at Jonesy's sweat-covered, frightened face to reassure him. He resisted the urge to look up at the wood car for help. The train slowed perceptibly not more than ten yards from the top.

Pat Kelly and Ben Adams had ridden the whole trip burrowed down in the wood car for protection from the winds. Neither of them thought seriously that there could be any danger on the trip. As soon as they had cleared Union Depot, they had thrown together a breastwork of wood against the wind and Adams had promptly fallen asleep. Kelly thought despairingly he had been put up here for no other reason than to keep him out of the way. He wondered what Adams had done to draw this assignment. Then he heard strange voices and he peered over the crudely constructed windbreak. His eyes flew open in surprise and he dug his elbow into Adams's side. Adams grunted, thinking a piece of wood had shifted and hit him. The look on Kelly's face told him otherwise.

Adams shifted his position to look over the wood, but in doing so he dislodged a stick that tumbled into the cab of the locomotive. He swore softly, but it was too late for that. The fat was in the fire.

Both Tader and Billy jerked around at the sound. All four

guns roared in unison as Kelly shouted at Adams above the noise.

"Look out, he's got dynamite!"

Tader was hit in the shoulder by Kelly's first shot. His own went zipping past the young Irishman's head, thrown off by Lucky Curtis, who grabbed the outlaw around the neck. Kelly hesitated for fear of hitting the engineer. Billy Hamill had traded a few shots with Adams without inflicting serious damage on either side. Hot lead clipped a piece of wood and sent splinters flying into the side of Adams's face. Jonesy cowered between the firebox and the steam jacket, unable to move.

Billy snapped another shot in the lawmen's direction and paused coolly to light one of the sticks of dynamite from the stub of his cigar. Adams stood up and fired point-blank into Billy. The shock sent the gunman reeling backward on top of the frightened Jonesy. The lit dynamite fell from Billy's hand and rolled into the narrow space separating the steam jacket and the floor of the locomotive.

Although mortally wounded, Billy thumbed back the hammer for a final time and shot Adams in the face. The security agent screamed in pain and Kelly turned to see Adams's face disintegrate into a red pulp.

Even with Lucky Curtis riding his neck, Tader managed to keep Kelly pinned down. The train engineer held to Tader with an iron grip, determined to throw him from the train.

Jonesy snapped out of his self-imposed shock and struggled frantically to free himself from beneath the dead outlaw after seeing the lighted dynamite roll beyond his grasp. His only chance was to jump . . . and quick. Kelly peered cautiously over the stack of wood into the smoke-filled locomotive. He saw Jonesy kick free and leap like a frightened pronghorn from the train at the instant the dynamite detonated.

Through the blast of the explosion the last thing Kelly saw was a solid sheet of red flame and white-hot steam rising up to engulf him. Caught in midair, the deafening blast sent Jonesy flying from the rails like a rock from a slingshot. His scalded and torn body landed some thirty feet away on the roadbed below, but there was no pain for Jonesy. Darkness descended on him before he hit the ground.

CHAPTER THIRTY-EIGHT

"My God! What was that?" Dillon asked, white-faced. Hunter regained his feet and hurried over to Jackson.

"They blew up the engine," Hunter replied grimly. Jackson sat slumped forward in the plush chair as blood from the three chest wounds stained the expensive fabric. His breathing was rapid and shallow. Hunter knelt before his friend.

"Danged if you weren't right, Jim," Jackson said weakly. He looked down between his legs at the fresh-lit cigar. "Hand me my cigar, will you?" He coughed, and the bright red liquid poured from his nose and mouth. He was drowning in his own blood and knew it. He looked at Hunter with pleading eyes filled with pain.

"Get the bastard, will you, Jim?" Hunter picked up the cigar.

"I will, Al, that's a promise." Jackson lowered his head and died. A black rage consumed Hunter. Another friend shot because of him. First Buck, now Jackson. He stood up, still holding the cigar. Grim-faced, Hunter punched out the spent shells and thumbed in new ones.

Henry Teller took the cigar from Hunter. "I'm real sorry about Jackson. If there's anything I can do . . . ?" Hunter shook his head and stepped onto the platform. Meekam was gone. He checked both sides of the train. Nothing. He spied Tolin sprawled out, still unconscious, and he yelled for Teller to tend to him once he checked Tolin for wounds. Up ahead, he could see the ominous black smoke and he wondered if young Kelly and Ben Adams had survived the blast. He knew the answer without thinking. Two more to add to his grim collection.

Hunter ran through the vacant news car and into total

confusion in the dining car. He shoved his way through the crowd, ignoring reporters' questions, and made his way into the cooking area. He found the cooks standing around, looking dazed and confused. Near the back entrance he found the wounded steward. Blood was pouring down the man's arm, which dangled at an awkward angle, indicating a broken bone.

"What happened here?" Hunter demanded. "You okay?"

"Yes, suh. Nuthin' but a scratch." The black man pointed to Quirt on the platform.

"Better have that arm tended to."

Hunter shouted to a small group of newsmen who crowded into the kitchen. "Few of you men with guns get up front and see if anyone needs help in the locomotive." Several weathered-faced individuals broke away and hurried forward, stepping around the prone Texan.

Hunter knelt beside Quirt and rolled him to his back. The outlaw's eyes were laced with pain.

"Hunter! Mighta known you'd survive. Third time we've met where there's been killing. Bad habit we got." He tried to smile but couldn't, the pain was so bad.

"What do you mean, third time?"

"The Wilderness with Uncle Louis . . . then Toby . . . and now me."

"You're dying, man. Tell me where Meekam is headed. The horses?"

"Go to hell!" Quirt said through the burning pain. Then he added, "Never figgered Meekam to pull through this. Means Grant is dead." Hunter shook his head.

"All the dying was for nothing. The President is safe in Black Hawk this very minute."

"You're lying," Quirt shot back, coughing up dark blood.

"Never lie to a dying man," Hunter said solemnly. Quirt saw the truth in Hunter's eyes, and he let his head fall back to the steel floor, too weak to hold it up anymore.

"Hunter," he whispered, "my name's Quirt Tyler, late of Alpine, Texas. See to it my paw gets my tack and whatever else. God, this place is cold." Death was not far away.

"I'll see to it." Quirt closed his eyes and mumbled something under his breath too low for Hunter to catch. He bent closer over the dying man.

"Said the horses are somewheres near the summit . . . Joe will be there." And then he died.

Hunter dropped off the train and headed forward through the black smoke that blotted out the sun. The air hung heavy with the smell of wood smoke, hot metal, and burning flesh. People from the train and from the road below milled about the charred wreckage in total confusion. Hunter holstered his gun as he walked slowly forward. Newsmen, with their instincts still intact, were throwing questions at anyone who stopped long enough for a few hasty words.

Hunter could not believe the destruction. The huge engine lay on its side like a giant beached whale, its inner steam jacket peeled back like a layer of blubber. Steaming metal littered the ground around the explosion area for some fifty feet or more. The front of the wood car was flattened, and smoldering wood smoke rose eerily from within the crushed blackened box. Adams and Kelly never had a chance, Hunter thought bitterly. A dark fury rose inside him as he started back down the tracks at a fast clip.

One thing he promised himself as he entered the presidential car—the killing stopped today. Teller and Dillon were gone and someone had draped a sheet over the bodies of Jackson and the dead outlaw. He stripped off the thin dress coat and pulled on his heavy winter coat. He turned to leave and hesitated. He stopped to pick up Grant's Sharps and a half box of shells. He had to act fast if he was going to stop Meekam before he got to the horses. He wondered how much time had elapsed. Ten, maybe twelve minutes tops, he figured.

Tolin stumbled through the door, holding his head. "Sorry, Jim. Never figured that angle."

"If it's any consolation, neither did I." Tolin sported a large goose egg, but he would survive.

"The others?" Tolin asked, looking down at the bloody sheet covering Jackson. Hunter shook his head.

"Get a wagon and take Teller and Dillon into Black Hawk and tell Nate to keep to the schedule. Nothing anyone can do here now. I'm headed after Meekam. If I'm lucky I'll meet him in Central City." Tolin stood still for a moment, looking at

Hunter. "Get a move on, Tolin." The lanky man bolted for the door.

Hunter stepped from the parlor car, and a dark spot he failed to notice before caught his eye. He bent down to examine the dark stain. Blood! So he hadn't missed Meekam after all. Maybe there was still time. He looked carefully in the snow and three steps away found another large stain. There were indentions as if Meekam were favoring one leg. The trail led upward toward the steep rocky summit.

Hunter began to climb the slippery loose rock as fast as he could. The heavy Sharps slowed him down somewhat. One thing was certain, if he ever got a clear shot at Meekam, he was going to take it without any warning.

Higher up, Meekam was making poor time with the leg wound. Even after he stuffed a bandanna into the open hole, blood still oozed out. The big slug had entered the thigh muscle and tunneled upward to lodge near the pelvic joint. The entry was less than two inches from where he had been shot by the Reb so long ago.

It hurt like hell and every step he made was pure agony. He gritted his teeth and continued to climb, oblivious to the arctic wind tearing at his thin coat. Several times he came close to fainting and was forced to stop until the giddiness left him. The crest of the summit was no more than a dozen yards away now.

It took Meekam another fifteen minutes to complete the climb, and once on top, he leaned heavily against a cold boulder to catch his breath in the thin air. He wasn't sure he had the strength to continue . . . or why. He had never planned beyond the point of killing Grant. Now that he was free, his only thought was to put some distance between himself and the train below. Meekam looked back at the smoky scene. Men scurried back and forth along the tracks like red ants on a dead animal. He looked at the gutted locomotive with grim satisfaction. Tader and Billy had done their job well. It was then he caught the movement some three hundred yards below him, and he studied the area carefully. The figure took shape, and Meekam recognized Hunter. He cursed bitterly. No matter. The law dog hadn't stopped him from putting three slugs in Grant. No man lived after those shots . . . not even a

Union general. He wished now he had listened to Quirt and disposed of Hunter when he had the chance.

His leg throbbed badly, and he knew he had to get to the horses before it got so bad he couldn't walk. Meekam turned away from the climbing Hunter and looked across the windswept landscape for a natural depression where the horses might be hidden. He nearly missed seeing them. They were in a draw some hundred yards away among large boulders and a few stunted trees. Meekam started toward them, dragging his stiffening leg. It took a while to cross the uneven rocky slope without falling, and he was completely winded when he finally reached them. They caught the scent of blood and bunched nervously. Meekam eased slowly forward. Already crippled, he didn't want to be kicked in the process. He reached out and caught the reins of a big roan. The horse tried to shy away.

"Steady, steady now," Meekam said soothingly as he untied the reins. It was all he could do to pull himself into the saddle, and he cried out in pain as he threw his injured leg over the horse. He sat there for a moment before he could see again through the pain.

What now? Which way should he go? The rocky draw was narrow and angled downslope, probably to the road leading into Black Hawk. No good. Place would be crawling with law dogs. He pointed the big roan north.

Hunter gained the summit in a third of the time it took Meekam. He quickly scanned the rocky area, breathing deeply in the thin, cold air. He spotted Meekam on the big horse some five hundred yards out, picking his way through a jumble of rock.

Today he had lost several good men, and possibly Buck, to this man, and now he aimed to even the score.

He flipped the sights up on the old breechloader and laid the heavy barrel across a boulder. He had never fired a Sharps before, much less at an object this far out. He sighted down the long barrel and adjusted for the slight rise between himself and Meekam. Meekam and the horse fit easily into the sights. He split the difference and squeezed the trigger.

The roar of the gun sent a solid jolt to Hunter's shoulder. The dull boom of the gun bounced off the rocky landscape and moved downslope. Hunter strained his eyes to see Meekam through the smoke. For a long moment he felt sure he had missed until the animal faltered and went down. Meekam fell or jumped clear of the horse. Hunter couldn't tell which.

Damn! He hated killing a good horse over the likes of Meekam. Hunter laid the Sharps on the rock. He would finish the job with his Colt. That he knew how to shoot.

Meekam was momentarily dazed by the fall, but the sharp pain in his leg jolted him back to reality. Blood was pouring from the leg wound again. This is it, Billy, he thought, looking up at the bright sky. "Hell, got no place to go anyway," he muttered. Billy smiled back through his pain. The image was crystal clear.

"You look fine, Billy," Meekam said softly to the wind. The vision faded at the sound of rocks rattling in the distance.

"That you, Hunter?" Meekam rolled to his belly and looked out between two rocks.

"I've come to send your soul to hell, Meekam!" A bullet chipped rock near Hunter's head. He rolled to his right and began inching forward on his stomach. "Unless you want to give yourself up."

"Go to hell! May as well die here as doing the air dance. Killing Grant ain't going to get me invited to no tea party." Hunter marked his position some fifty yards away.

"You didn't kill the President, Meekam," Hunter called back, then added softly to himself, "Only a friend."

"You're lying, Yank," Meekam screamed. "Saw him take three of my slugs, so don't try that crap with me." Meekam fired two shots that went wide of where Hunter lay. Meekam's vision blurred some as he put fresh shells in his gun.

"It was a double . . . a trick." Meekam ran his hands over his eyes, trying to clear them. Hunter had to be lying. Or was he? Then it struck him? Something had bothered him about that guard; now, he feared, he knew why. For someone who was supposed to be guarding the President, he acted too relaxed, unconcerned. And what was it he had said? "'Bout time. You got a bunch of hungry fellows over there." He hadn't referred to Grant at all. Bitterness welled in his throat and unbridled fury shook him to the core. He turned his hatred

188

toward Hunter for taking away the only thing that mattered in his life.

"Hunter. Damn you and Grant!" Meekam screamed as he flung himself into an awkward stance and began firing wildly in Hunter's direction.

Hunter felt the well-balanced Colt buck twice. It was all that was needed. The heart shots flung Meekam backward into the rocks. He died with a half-smile on his lips and a fading vision of a young boy in a suit of ill-fitting clothes.

An hour later a gleaming carriage pulled up to the Teller House in Central City, where a crowd watched as the President of the United States alighted to walk across a sidewalk laid with shining silver ingots from the Caribou Mine to take the hand of the manager, Bill Bush. The President was flanked on his right by a big man dressed in black who continuously swept the enthusiastic crowd with pale, cold eyes.

CHAPTER THIRTY-NINE

Nate Gage leaned against a post in front of Potter's Mercantile with his black hat pushed to the back of his head and watched with faint amusement as Hunter tied several packages to the wide-shouldered chestnut he had just purchased.

The smell of spring was on the wind despite the steadily falling silver-dollar-size snowflakes.

"Weather's going to make it rough crossing those mountain passes," Gage volunteered. Hunter looked up from under the brim of his low-pulled hat and studied the big man for a moment. He was going to miss Gage. They had been through a lot together these past fifteen years: the bloody Civil War; doing their part as members of the Watchers to protect General Grant; and the tough times following Lincoln's assassination when they both came close to resigning from the secret service but for the wisdom of a man named Hiram Ulysses Grant.

"Passes won't be so bad," Hunter remarked. "Out here you learn to live with everything the mountains throw at you. Kinda like riding in the snow. Clears the senses, like the first streaks of early morning washing away the night." Gage struck a match and lit a thin cigar. He looked at his friend through the blue haze.

"Won't change your mind?" Hunter shook his head slowly and checked the cinch before pulling himself into the saddle. The big horse shifted nervously beneath him as if anticipating the long ride. He curbed the animal's energy.

"What would I do with the dress and set of leathers I just bought? Seriously, Nate. I'm tired of the city, and especially the killing. I belong out here now. Will you come for a visit?"

"Reckon so . . . someday. If this Gunnison country is everything you say it is, I just might carve out a piece for myself and settle down."

Hunter walked the chestnut over to the edge of the boardwalk and extended his hand: "I've said my good-byes to the President. You're the best friend a man could ever hope to have in one lifetime." They shook hands firmly. Gage's face ▮bered.

"Jim . . . with you at my side I never worried about my back. Good luck." Hunter knew he had just been paid the highest compliment Gage was capable of.

"Luck to you, Nathaniel." Hunter turned down Gregory ▮eet and eased the willing horse into a ground-eating canter.

For a few brief moments a rider was outlined on a ridge ab▮ve a narrow valley as he studied the small cabin far below. A ▮hin trail of smoke drifted upward in the warm spring air from the chimney. The sharp cry of an eagle floated up to the rider as ▮e big bird circled the canyon, riding the warm updrafts. The ▮er put spurs to the big horse.

In a short while the rider walked his horse across the swift creek and up to the cabin door.

Hunter was dismounting when the door flew open and Jay rushed outside, wide-eyed and happy. She stopped abruptly, her face flushed. Hunter's heart was pounding so hard against his ribs he could barely speak.

"Jay, I—" The next thing he knew, Jay was in his arms and they were kissing. They pulled back from each other after a while and Hunter looked at her questioningly.

"He's going to be all right, Jim." Relief washed over him, and Hunter hugged her to him once more. He wasn't sure he could have taken Buck dying too.

"I love you, Jay."

Jay smiled shyly at him and tweaked his nose playfully. "I've always known that, silly."

"Here now, no time fer that. A fellar in my condition could

191

die afore he ever sets another trap on the Gunnison. Get to packin', gal!"

Hunter looked over Jay's shoulder and his face broke into a wide grin at the sight of the old mountain man standing in the doorway. He had lost a lot of weight but none of his wit.

"Buck, it sure is good to see you again."